ABSALOM'S HAIR

LECTOR HOUSE PUBLIC DOMAIN WORKS

ABSALOM'S HAIR

BJORNSTJERNE BJORNSON

ISBN: 978-93-5344-011-4

First Published: -

LECTOR HOUSE LLP
E-MAIL: lectorpublishing@gmail.com

ABSALOM'S HAIR

BY

BJORNSTJERNE BJORNSON

CONTENTS

CHAPTER 1

Harald Kaas was sixty.

He had given up his free, uncriticised bachelor life; his yacht was no longer seen off the coast in summer; his tours to England and the south had ceased; nay, he was rarely to be found even at his club in Christiania. His gigantic figure was never seen in the doorways; he was failing.

Bandy-legged he had always been, but this defect had increased; his herculean back was rounded, and he stooped a little. His forehead, always of the broadest—no one else's hat would fit him—was now one of the highest, that is to say, he had lost all his hair, except a ragged lock over each ear and a thin fringe behind. He was beginning also to lose his teeth, which were strong though small, and blackened by tobacco; and now, instead of "deuce take it" he said "deush take it."

He had always held his hands half closed as though grasping something; now they had stiffened so that he could never open them fully. The little finger of his left hand had been bitten off "in gratitude" by an adversary whom he had knocked down: according to Harald's version of the story, he had compelled the fellow to swallow the piece on the spot.

He was fond of caressing the stump, and it often served as an introduction to the history of his exploits, which became greater and greater as he grew older and quieter.

His small sharp eyes were deep set and looked at one with great intensity. There was power in his individuality, and, besides shrewd sense, he possessed a considerable gift for mechanics. His boundless self-esteem was not devoid of greatness, and the emphasis with which both body and soul proclaimed themselves made him one of the originals of the country.

Why was he nothing more?

He lived on his estate, Hellebergene, whose large woods skirted the coast, while numerous leasehold farms lay along the course of the river. At one time this estate had belonged to the Kurt family, and had now come back to them, in so far as that Harald's father, as every one knew, was not a Kaas at all, but a Kurt; it was he who had got the estate together again; a book might be written about the ways and means that he had employed.

The house looked out over a bay studded with islands; farther out were more islands and the open sea. An immensely long building, raised on an old and massive foundation, its eastern wing barely half furnished, the western inhabited by Harald Kaas, who lived his curious life here.

These wings were connected by two covered galleries, one above the other, with stairs at each end.

Curiously enough, these galleries did not face the sea, that is, the south, but the fields and woods to the north. The portion of the house between the two wings was a neutral territory—namely, a large dining-room with a ballroom above it, neither of which was used in later years.

Harald Kaas's suite of rooms was distinguished from without by a mighty elk's head with its enormous antlers, which was set up over the gallery.

In the gallery itself were heads of bear, wolf, fox and lynx, with stuffed birds from land and sea. Skins and guns hung on the walls of the anteroom, the inner rooms were also full of skins and impregnated with the smell of wild animals and tobacco-smoke. Harald himself called it "Man-smell;" no one who had once put his nose inside could ever forget it.

Valuable and beautiful skins hung on the walls and covered the floors; his very bed was nothing else; Harald Kaas lay, and sat, and walked on skins, and each one of them was a welcome subject of conversation, for he had shot and flayed every single animal himself. To be sure, there were those who hinted that most of the skins had been bought from Brand and Company, of Bergen, and that only the stories were shot and flayed at home.

I for my part think that this was an exaggeration; but be that as it may, the effect was equally thrilling when Harald Kaas, seated in his log chair by the fireside, his feet on the bearskin, opened his shirt to show us the scars on his hairy chest (and what scars they were!) which had been made by the bear's teeth, when he had driven his knife, right up to the haft, into the monster's heart. All the queer tankards, and cupboards, and carved chairs listened with their wonted impassiveness.

Harald Kaas was sixty, when, in the month of July, he sailed into the bay accompanied by four ladies whom he had brought from the steamer—an elderly lady and three young ones, all related to him. They were to stay with him until August.

They occupied the upper storey. From it they could hear him walking about and grunting below them. They began to feel a little nervous. Indeed, three of them had had serious misgivings about accepting the invitation; and these misgivings were not diminished when, next morning, they saw Kaas composedly strolling up from the sea stark naked!

They screamed, and, gathering together, still in their nightgowns, held a council of war as to the advisability of leaving at once; but when one of them cried "You should not have called us, Aunt, and then we should not have seen him," they could not help laughing, and therewith the whole affair ended. Certainly they were a little stiff at breakfast; but when Harold Kaas began a story about an old black mare of his which was in love with a young brown horse over at the Dean's, and which plunged madly if any other horse came near her, but, on the other hand, put her head coaxingly on one side and whinnied "like a dainty girl" whenever the parson's horse came that way—well, at that they had to give in, as well first as last.

If they had strayed here out of curiosity they must just put up with the "NIGHT side of nature," as Harald Kaas expressed it, with the stress on the first word.

For all that they were nearly frightened out of their wits the very next night, when he discharged his gun right under their windows. The aunt even asserted that he had shot through her open casement. She screamed loudly, and the others, starting from their sleep, were out on the floor before they knew where they were. Then they crouched in the windows and peeped out, although their aunt declared that they would certainly be shot—they really must see what it was.

Yes! there they saw him among the cherry and apple trees, gun in hand, and they could hear him swearing. In the greatest trepidation they crept back into bed again. Next morning they learned that he had shot at some night prowlers, one of whom had got "half the charge in his leg, that he had, Deush take him! It ain't the prowling I mind, but that he should prowl here. We bachelors will have no one poaching on our preserves."

The four ladies sat as stiff as four church candles, till at length one of them sprang up with a scream, the others joining in chorus.

The visitors were not bored; Harald Kaas dealt too much in the unexpected for that. There was a charm, too, in the great woods, where there had been no felling since he had come into the property, and there were merry walks by the riverside and plenty of fish in the river.

They bathed, they took delightful sails in the cutter and drives about the neighbourhood, though certainly the turn-out was none of the smartest.

The youngest of the girls, Kristen Ravn, presently became less eager to join in these expeditions. She had fallen in love with the disused east wing of the house, and there she spent many a long hour, alone by the open window, gazing out at the great lime-trees which stood straggling, gaunt, and mysterious.

"You ought to build a balcony here, out towards the sea," she said. "Look how the water glitters between the limes."

When once she had hit upon a plan, Kristen Ravn never relinquished it, and when she had suggested it some four or five times, he promised that it should be done. But on the heels of this scheme came another.

"Below the first balcony there must be another wider one," said she in her soft voice, "and it must have steps at each end down to the lawn—the lawn is so lovely just here."

The unheard-of presumption of her demand inoculated him with the idea, and at length he consented to this as well.

"The rooms must be refurnished," she gravely commanded. "The one next to the balcony which is to be built under here shall be in yellow pine, and the floor must be polished." She pointed with her long delicate hand. "ALL the floors must be polished. I will give you the design for the room above, I have thought it carefully out." And in imagination she papered the walls, arranged the furniture, and hung up curtains of wondrous patterns.

"I know, too, how the other rooms are to be done," she added. And she went from one to the other, remaining a little while in each. He followed, like an old horse led by the bridle.

Before their visit was half over he most coolly neglected three out of his four guests.

His deep-set eyes twinkled with the liveliest admiration whenever she approached. He sought in the faces of the others the admiration which he himself felt: he would amble round her like an old photographic camera which had the power of setting itself up.

But from the day when she took down from his bookshelf a French work on mechanics, a subject with which she was evidently acquainted and for which she declared that she had a natural aptitude, it was all over with him. From that day forward, if she were present, he effaced himself both in word and action.

In the mornings when he met her in one of her characteristic costumes he laughed softly, or gazed and gazed at her, and then glanced towards the others. She did not talk much, but every word that she uttered aroused his admiration. But he was most of all captivated when she sat quietly apart, heedless of every one: at such times he resembled an old parrot expectant of sugar.

His linen had always been snowy white, but beyond this he had taken no special pains with his toilet; but now he strutted about in a Tussore silk coat, which he had bought in Algiers, but had at once put aside because it was too tight—he looked like a clipt box hedge in it.

Now, who was this lion-tamer of twenty-one, who, without in the least wishing to do so, unconsciously even (she was the quietest of the party), had made the monarch of the forest crouch at her feet and gaze at her in abject humility?

Look at her, as she sits there, with her loose shining hair of the prettiest shade of dark red; look at her broad forehead and prominent nose, but more than all at those large wondering eyes; look at her throat and neck, her tall slight figure; notice especially the Renaissance dress which she wears, its style and colour, and your curiosity will still remain unsatisfied, for she has an individuality all her own.

Kristen Ravn had lost her mother at her birth and her father when she was five years old. The latter left her a handsome fortune, with the express condition that the investments should not be changed, and that the income should be for her own use whether she married or not. He hoped by this means to form her character. She was brought up by three different members of her wide-branching family, a family which might more properly be termed a clan, although they had no common characteristics beyond a desire to go their own way.

When two Ravns meet they, as a rule, differ on every subject; but as a race they hold religiously together—indeed, in their eyes there is no other family which is "amusing," the favourite adjective of the Ravns.

Kristen had a receptive nature; she read everything, and remembered what she read; that is say, she had a logical mind, for a retentive memory implies an orderly brain. She was consequently NUMBER ONE in everything which she took up. This, coupled with the fact that she lived among those who regarded her somewhat as a speculation, and consequently flattered her, had early made an impression on her nature, quite as great, indeed, as the possession of money.

She was by no means proud, it was not in the Ravn nature to be so; but at ten years old she had left off playing; she preferred to wander in the woods and compose ballads. At twelve she insisted on wearing silk dresses, and, in the teeth of an aunt all curls and lace and with a terrible flow of words, she carried her point. She held herself erect and prim in her silks, and still remained NUMBER ONE. She composed verses about Sir Adge and Maid Else, about birds and flowers and sad things.

On reaching the age at which other girls, who have the means, begin to wear silk dresses, she left them off. She was tired, she said, of the "smooth and glossy."

She now grew enthusiastic for fine wool and expensive velvet of every shade. Dresses in the Renaissance style became her favourites, and the subject of her studies. She puffed out her bodices like those in Leonardo's and Rafael's portraits of women, and tried in other ways as well to resemble them.

She left off writing verses, and wrote stories instead; the style was good, though they were anything rather than spontaneous.

They were short, with a more or less clear pointe. Stories by a girl of eighteen do not as a general rule make a sensation, but these were particularly audacious. It was evident that their only object was to scandalise. Instead of her own name she used the nom-de-plume of "Puss." This, however, was only to postpone the announcement that the author who scandalised her readers most, and that at a time when every author strove to do so, was a girl of eighteen belonging to one of the first families in the country.

Soon every one knew that "Puss" was she of the tumbled red locks, "the tall Renaissance figure with the Titian hair."

Her hair was abundant, glossy, and slightly curling; she still wore it hanging loose over her neck and shoulders, as she had done as a child. Her great eyes seemed to look out upon a new world; but one felt that the lower part of her face was scarcely in harmony with the upper. The cheeks fell in a little; the prominent nose made the mouth look smaller than it actually was; her neck seemed only to lead the eye downward to her bosom, which almost appeared to caress her throat, especially when her head was bent forward, as was generally the case. And very beautiful the throat was, delicate in colour, superb in contour, and admirably set upon the bust. For this reason she could never find in her heart to hide this full white neck, but always kept it uncovered. Her finely moulded bust surmounting a slender waist and small hips, her rounded arms, her long hands, her graceful carriage, in her tightly-fitting dress, formed such a striking picture that one did more than look—one was obliged to study her, When the elegance and beauty of her dress were taken into account, one realised how much intelligence and artistic taste had here been exercised.

She was friendly in society, natural and composed, always occupied with something, always with that wondering expression. She spoke very little, but her words were always well chosen.

All this, and her general disposition, made people chary of opposing her, more especially those who knew how intelligent she was and how much knowledge she possessed.

She had no friends of her own, but her innumerable relations supplied her with society, gossip, and flattery, and were at once her friends and body-guard. She would have had to go abroad to be alone.

Among these relations she was a princess: they not only paid her homage, but had sworn by "Life and Death" that she must marry without more ado, which was absolutely against her wish.

From her childhood she had been laying by money, but the amount of her savings was far less than her relations supposed. This rather mythical fortune contributed not a little to the fact that "every one" was in love with her. Not only the bachelors of the family, that was a matter of course, but artists and amateurs, even the most blase, swarmed round her, la jeunesse doree (which is homely enough in Norway), without an exception. A living work of art, worth more or less money, piquante and admired, how each longed to carry her home, to gloat over her, to call her his own!

There was surely more intensity of feeling near her than near others, a losing of oneself in one only; that unattainable dream of the world-weary.

With her one could lead a thoroughly stylish life, full of art and taste and comfort. She was highly cultivated, and absolutely emancipated—our little country did not, in those days, possess a more alluring expression.

When face to face with her they were uncertain how to act, whether to approach her diffidently or boldly, smile or look serious, talk or be silent.

What these idle wooers gleaned from her stories, her characteristic dress, her wondering eyes, and her quiet dreaminess, was not the highest, but they expended their energy thereon; so that their unbounded discomfiture may be imagined when, in the autumn, the news spread that Fruken Kristen Ravn was married to Harald Kaas.

They burst into peals of derisive laughter they scoffed, they exclaimed; the only explanation they could offer was that they had too long hesitated to try their fortune.

There were others, who both knew and admired her, who were no less dismayed. They were more than disappointed—the word is too weak; to many of them it seemed simply deplorable. How on earth could it have happened? Every one, herself excepted, knew that it would ruin her life.

On Kristen Ravn's independent position, her strong character, her rare courage, on her knowledge, gifts, and energy, many, especially women, had built up a future for the cause of Woman. Had she not already written fearlessly for it? Her tendency towards eccentricity and paradox would soon have worn off, they thought, as the struggle carried her forward, and at last she might have become one of the first champions of the cause. All that was noblest and best in Kristen must predominate in the end.

And now the few who seek to explain life's perplexities rather than to condemn them discovered—Some of them, that the defiant tone of her writings and her love of opposition bespoke a degree of vanity sufficient to have led her into fallacy. Others maintained that hers was essentially a romantic nature which might cause her to form a false estimate both of her own powers and of the circumstances of life. Others, again, had heard something of how this husband and wife lived, one in each wing of the house, with different staffs of servants, and with separate incomes; that she had furnished her side in her own way, at her own expense, and had apparently conceived the idea of a new kind of married life. Some people declared that the great lime-trees near the mansion at Hellebergene were alone responsible for the marriage. They soughed so wondrously in the summer evenings, and the sea beneath their branches told such enthralling stories. Those grand old woods, the like of which were hardly to be found in impoverished Norway, were far dearer to her than was her husband. Her imagination had been taken captive by the trees, and thus Harald Kaas had taken HER. The estate, the climate, the exclusive possession of her part of the house: this was the bait which she had chosen. Harald Kaas was only a kind of Puck who had to be taken along with it. But it is doubtful whether this conjecture was any nearer the truth. No one ever really knew. She was not one of those whom it is easy to catechise.

Every one wearies at last of trying to solve even the most interesting of enigmas. No one could tolerate the sound of her name when, four months after her marriage, she was seen in a stall at the Christiania Theatre just as in old days, though looking perhaps a little paler. Every opera-glass was levelled at her. She wore a light, almost white, dress, cut square as usual. She did not hide her face behind her fan. She looked about her with her wondering eyes, as though she was quite unconscious that there were other people in the theatre or that any one could be looking at her. Even the most pertinacious were forced to concede that she was both physically and mentally unique, with a charm all her own.

But just as she had become once more the subject of general conversation, she disappeared. It afterwards transpired that her husband had fetched her away, though hardly any one had seen him. It was concluded that they must have had their first quarrel over it.

Accurate information about their joint life was never obtained. The attempts of her relations to force themselves upon them were quite without result, except that they found out that she was enceinte, notwithstanding her utmost efforts to conceal the fact.

She sent neither letter nor announcement; but in the summer, when she was next seen in Christiania, she was wheeling a perambulator along Karl Johan Street, her eyes as wondering as though some one had just put it between her hands. She looked handsomer and more blooming than ever.

In the perambulator lay a boy with his mother's broad forehead, his mother's red hair. The child was charmingly dressed, and he, as well as the perambulator, was so daintily equipped, so completely in harmony with herself, that every one understood the reply that she gave, when, after the usual congratulations, her acquaintances inquired, "Shall we soon have a new story from you?"—she answered, "A new story? Here it is!"

But, notwithstanding the unalloyed happiness which she displayed here, it could no longer be concealed that more often than not she was absent from home, and that she never mentioned her husband's name. If any one spoke of him to her, she changed the subject. By the time that the boy was a year old, it had become evident that she contemplated leaving Hellebergene entirely. She had been in Christiania for some time and had gone home to make arrangements, saying that she should come back in a few days.

But she never did so.

The day after her return home, while the numerous servants at Hellebergene, as well as the labourers with their wives and children, were all assembled at the potato digging, Harald Kaas appeared, carrying his wife under his left arm like a sack. He held her round the waist, feet first, her face downwards and hidden by her hair, her hands convulsively clutching his left thigh, her legs sometimes hanging down, sometimes straight out. He walked composedly out with her, holding in his right hand a bunch of long fresh birch twigs. A little way from the gallery he paused, and laying her across his left knee, he tore off some of her clothes, and beat her until the blood flowed. She never uttered a sound. When he put her from him, she tremblingly rearranged—first her hair, thus displaying her face just as the blood flowed back from it, leaving it deadly white. Tears of pain and shame rolled down her cheeks; but still not a sound. She tried to rearrange her dress, but her tattered garments trailed behind her as she went back to the house. She shut the door after her, but had to open it again; her torn clothes had caught fast in it.

The women stood aghast; some of the children screamed with fright: this infected the rest, and there was a chorus of sobs. The men, most of whom had been sitting smoking their pipes, but who had sprung to their feet again, stood filled with shame and indignation.

It had not been without a pang that Harald Kaas had done this, his face and manner had shown it for a long time and still did so; but he had expected that a roar of laughter would greet his extraordinary vagary. This was evident from the composure with which he had carried his wife out; and still more from the glance of gratified revenge with which he looked round him afterwards. But there was only dead stillness, succeeded by weeping, sobbing, and indignation. He stood there for a moment, quite overcome, then went indoors again, a defeated, utterly broken man.

In every encounter with this delicate creature the giant had been worsted.

After this, however, she never went beyond the grounds. For the first few years she was only seen by the people about the estate, and by them but seldom. Sometimes she would take her boy out in his little carriage, or, as time went on, would lead him by the hand, sometimes she was alone. She was generally wrapped in a big shawl, a different one for each dress she wore, and which she always held tightly round her. This was so characteristic of her that to this day I hear people from the neighbourhood talk about it as though she were never seen otherwise.

What then did she do? She studied; she had given up writing: for more than one reason it had become distasteful to her. She had changed roles with her husband, giving herself up to mathematics, chemistry, and physics, she made calculations and analyses—sending for books and materials for these objects. The people on the estate saw nothing extraordinary in all this. From the first they had admired her delicacy and beauty. Every one admired her; it was only the manner and degree that varied.

Little by little she came to be regarded as one whose life and thoughts were beyond their comprehension.

She sought no one, but to those who came to her she never refused help—more or less. She made herself well acquainted with the facts of each case; no one could ever deceive her. Whether she gave much or little, she imposed no conditions, she never lectured them. Her opinion was expressed by the amount that she gave.

Her husband's behaviour towards her was such that, had she not been very popular, she could not have remained at Hellebergene; that is to say, he opposed and thwarted her in every way he could; but every one took her part.

The boy! Could not he have been a bond of union? On the contrary, there were those who declared that it was from the time of his birth that things had gone amiss between the parents. The first time that his father saw him the nurse reported that he "came in like a lord and went out like a beggar!" The mother lay down again and laughed; the nurse had never seen the like of it before. Had he expected that his child must of necessity resemble him, only to find it the image of its mother?

When the boy was old enough he loved to wander across to his father's rooms where there were so many curious things to see; his father always received him kindly, talking in a way suited to his childish intelligence, but he would take occasion to cut away a quantity of his hair. His mother let it grow free and long like her own, and his father perpetually cut it. The boy would have been glad enough to be rid of it, but when he grew a little older, he comprehended his father's motive, and thenceforth he was on his guard.

When the people on the estate had told him something of his father's highly-coloured histories of his feats of strength and his achievements by land and water, the boy began to feel a shy admiration for him, but at the same time he felt all the more strongly the intolerable yoke which he laid upon them—upon every living being on the estate. It became a secret religion with him to oppose his father and help his mother, for it was she who suffered. He would resemble her even to his hair, he would protect her, he would make it all up to her. It was a positive delight to him when his father made him suffer: he absolutely felt proud when he called him Rafaella, instead of Rafael, the name which his mother had chosen for him; it was the one that she loved best.

No one was allowed to use the boats or the carriage, no one might walk through the woods, which had been fenced in, the horses were never taken out. No repairs were undertaken; if Fru Kaas attempted to have anything done at her own expense, the workmen were ordered off: there could no longer be any doubt about it, he wished everything to go to rack and ruin. The property went from bad to worse, and the woods—well! It was no secret, every one on the place talked about it—the timber was being utterly ruined. The best and largest trees were already rotten; by degrees the rest would become so.

At twelve years of age Rafael began to receive religious teaching from the Dean: the only subject in which his mother did not instruct him. He shared these lessons with Helene, the Dean's only child, who was four years younger than Rafael and of whom he was devotedly fond.

The Dean told them the story of David. The narrative was unfolded with additions and explanations; the boy made a picture of it to himself; his mother had taught him everything in this way.

Assyrian warriors with pointed beards, oblique eyes, and oblong shields, had to represent the Israelites; they marched by in an endless procession. He saw the blue-green of the vineyards on the hillside, the shadow of the dusty palm-trees upon the dusty road. Then a wood of aromatic trees into which all the warriors fled.

Then followed the story of Absalom.

"Absalom rebelled against his father, what a dreadful thing to think of," said the Dean. "A grown-up man to rebel against his father." He chanced to look towards Rafael, who turned as red as fire.

The thought which was constantly in his mind was that when he was grown up he should rebel against his father.

"But Absalom was punished in a marvellous manner," continued the Dean. "He lost the battle, and as he fled through the woods, his long hair caught in a tree, the horse ran away from under him, and he was left hanging there until he was run through by a spear."

Rafael could see Absalom hanging there, not in the long Assyrian garments, not with a pointed beard. No! Slender and young, in Rafael's tight-fitting breeches and stockings, and with his own red hair! Ah! how distinctly he saw it! The horse galloping far away—the grey one at home which he used to ride by stealth when his father was asleep after dinner. He could see the tall, slender lad, dangling and swaying, with a spear through his body. Distinctly! Distinctly!

This vision, which he never mentioned to a soul, he could not get rid of. To be left hanging there by his hair—what a strange punishment for rebelling against his father!

Certainly he already knew the history, but till now he had paid no special heed to it.

It was on a Friday that this great impression had been made on him, and on the following Thursday morning he awoke to see his mother standing over him with her most wondering expression. Her hair still as she had plaited it for the night; one plait had touched him on the nose and awoke him before she spoke. She stood bending over him, in her long white nightgown with its dainty lace trimming, and with bare feet. She would never have come in like that if something terrible had not happened. Why did she not speak? only look and look—or was she really frightened?

"Mother!" he cried, sitting up.

Then she bent close down to him. "THE MAN IS DEAD," she whispered. It was his father whom she called "the man," she never spoke of him otherwise.

Rafael did not comprehend what she said, or perhaps it paralysed him. She repeated it again louder and louder, "The man is dead, the man is dead."

Then she stood upright, and putting out her bare feet from under her night-gown, she began to dance—only a few steps; and then she slipped away through the door which stood half open. He jumped up and ran after her; there she lay on the sofa, sobbing. She felt that he was behind her, she raised herself quickly, and, still sobbing, pressed him to her heart.

Even when they stood together beside the body, the hand which he had in his shook so that he threw his arms round her, thinking that she would fall.

Later in life, when he recalled this, he understood what she had silently endured, what an unbending will she had brought to the struggle, but also what it had cost her.

At the time he did not in the least comprehend it. He imagined that she suffered from the horror of the moment as he himself did.

There lay the giant, in wretchedness and squalor! He who had once boasted of his cleanliness, and expected the like in others, lay there, dirty and unshaven, under dirty bed clothes, in linen so ragged and filthy that no workman on the estate had worse. The clothes which he had worn the day before lay on a chair beside the bed, miserably threadbare, foul with dirt, sweat, and tobacco, and stinking like everything else. His mouth was distorted, his hands tightly clenched; he had died of a stroke.

And how forlorn and desolate was all around him! Why had his son never noticed this before? Why had he never felt that his father was lonely and forsaken? To how great an extent no words could express.

Rafael burst into tears; louder and louder grew his sobbing, until it sounded through all the rooms. The people from the estate came in one by one. They wished to satisfy their curiosity.

The boy's crying, unconsciously to himself, influenced them all: they saw everything in a new light. How unfortunate, how desolate, how helpless had he been who now lay there. Lord, have mercy on us all!

When the corpse of Harald Kaas had been laid out, the face shaved, and the eyes closed, the distortion was less apparent. They could trace signs of suffering, but the expression was still virile. It seemed a handsome face to them now.

CHAPTER 2

Within a few days of the funeral mother and son were in England.

Rafael was now to enter upon a long course of study, for which, by his earlier education, his mother had prepared him, and for which, by painful privations, she had saved up sufficient money.

The property was to the last degree impoverished, and burdened with mortgages, and the timber only fit for fuel.

Their neighbour the Dean, a clear-headed and practical man, took upon himself the management of affairs; as money was needed the work of devastation must begin at once. The mother and son did not wish to witness it.

They came to England like two fugitives who, after many and great trials, for affection's sake seek a new home and a new country.

Rafael was then twelve years old.

They were inseparable, and in the shiftless life that they led in their new surroundings they became, if possible, more closely attached to each other.

Yet not long afterwards they had their first disagreement.

He had gone to school, had begun to learn the language and to make friends, and had developed a great desire to show off.

He was very tall and slender and was anxious to be athletic. He took an active part in the play-ground, but here he achieved no great success. On the other hand, thanks to his mother, he was better informed than his comrades, and he contrived to obtain prominence by this. This prominence must be maintained, and nothing answered so well as boasting about Norway and his father's exploits. His statements were somewhat exaggerated, but that was not altogether his fault, He knew English fairly well, but had not mastered its niceties. He made use of superlatives, which always come the most readily. It was true that he had inherited from his father twenty guns, a large sailing-boat, and several smaller ones; but how magnificent these boats and guns had become!

He intended to go to the North Pole, he said, as his father had done, to shoot white bears, and invited them all to come with him.

He made a greater impression on his hearers than he himself was aware of; but something more was wanted, for it was impossible to foretell from day to day what might be expected of him. He had to study hard in order to meet the demand.

As an outcome of this, he betook himself one evening to the hairdresser's, with some of his schoolfellows, and, without more ado, requested him to cut his hair quite close. That ought to satisfy them for a long time.

The other boys had teased him about his hair, and it got in the way when he was playing—he hated it. Besides, ever since the story of Absalom's rebellion and punishment, it had remained a secret terror to him, but it had never before occurred to him to have it cut off.

His schoolfellows were dismayed, and the hairdresser looked on it as a work of wilful destruction.

Rafael felt his heart begin to sink, but the very audacity of the thing gave him courage They should see what he dare do. The hairdresser hesitated to act without Fru Kaas's knowledge, but at length he ceased to make objections.

Rafael's heart sank lower and lower, but he must go through with it now. "Off with it," he said, and remained immovable in the chair.

"I have never seen more splendid hair," said the hairdresser diffidently, taking up the scissors but still hesitating.

Rafael saw that his companions were on the tiptoe of expectation. "Off with it," he said again with assumed indifference.

The hairdresser cut the hair into his hand and laid it carefully in paper.

The boys followed every snip of the scissors with their eyes, Rafael with his ears; he could not see in the glass.

When the hairdresser had finished and had brushed his clothes for him, he offered him the hair. "What do I want with it?" said Rafael. He dusted his elbows and knees a little, paid, and left the shop, followed by his companions. They, however, exhibited no particular admiration. He caught a glimpse of himself in the glass as he went out, and thought that he looked frightful.

He would have given all that he possessed (which was not much), he would have endured any imaginable suffering, he thought, to have his hair back again.

His mother's wondering eyes rose up before him with every shade of expression; his misery pursued him, his vanity mocked him. The end of it all was that he stole up to his room and went to bed without his supper.

But when his mother had vainly waited for him, and some one suggested that he might be in the house, she went to his room.

He heard her on the stairs; he felt that she was at the door. When she entered he had hidden his head beneath the bedclothes. She dragged them back; and at the first sight of her dismay he was reduced to such despair that the tears which were beginning to flow ceased at once.

White and horror-struck she stood there; indeed she thought at first that some one had done it maliciously; but when she could not extract a word of enlightenment, she suspected mischief.

He felt that she was waiting for an explanation, an excuse, a prayer for forgiveness, but he could not, for the life of him, get out a word.

What, indeed, could he say? He did not understand it himself. But now he began to cry violently. He huddled himself together, clasping his head between his hands. It felt like a bristly stubble.

When he looked up again his mother was gone.

A child sleeps in spite of everything. He came down the next morning in a contrite mood and thoroughly shamefaced. His mother was not up; she was unwell, for she had not slept a wink. He heard this before he went to her. He opened her door timidly. There she lay, the picture of wretchedness.

On the toilet-table, in a white silk handkerchief, was his hair, smoothed and combed.

She lay there in her lace-trimmed nightgown, great tears rolling down her cheeks. He had come, intending to throw himself into her arms and beg her pardon a thousand times. But he had a strong feeling that he had better not do so, or was he afraid to? She was in the clouds, far, far away. She seemed in a trance: something, at once painful and sacred, held her enchained. She was both pathetic and sublime.

The boy stepped quietly from the room and hurried off to school.

She remained in bed that day and the next, and made him sit with the servant in order that she might be alone. When she was in trouble she always behaved thus, and that he should cross her in this way was the greatest trial that she had ever known. It came upon her, too, like a deluge of rain from a clear sky. NOW it seemed to her that she could foresee his future—and her own.

She laid the blame of all this on his paternal ancestry. She could not see that incessant artistic fuss and too much intellectual training had, perhaps, aroused in him a desire for independence.

The first time that she saw him again with his cropped head, which grew more and more like his father's in shape, her tears flowed quietly.

When he wished to come to her side, she waived him back with her shapely hand, nor would she talk to him; when he talked she hardly looked at him; till at last he burst into tears. For he suffered as one can suffer but once, when the childish penitence is fresh and therefore boundless, and when the yearning for love has received its first rebuff.

But when, on the fifth day, she met him coming up the stairs, she stood still in dismay at his appearance: pale, thin, timid; the effect perhaps heightened by the loss of his hair. He, too, stood still, looking forlorn and abject, with disconsolate eyes. Then hers filled; she stretched out her arms. He was once more in his Paradise, but they both cried as though they must wade through an ocean of tears before they could talk to each other again.

"Tell me about it now," she whispered. This was in her own room. They had spoken the first fond words and kissed each other over and over again. "How could this have happened, Rafael?" she whispered again, with her head pressed to his; she did not wish to look at him while she spoke.

"Mother," he answered, "it is worse to cut down the woods at home, at Helle-bergene, than that I—"

She raised her head and looked at him. She had taken off her hat and gloves, but now she put them quickly on again.

"Rafael, dear," she said, "shall we go for a walk together in the park, under the grand old trees?"

She had felt his retort to be ingenious.

After this episode, however, England, and more especially her son's schoolfellows, became distasteful to her, and she constantly made plans to keep him away from the latter out of school hours.

She found this very easy; sometimes she went over his studies with him, at others they visited all the Manufactories and "Works" for miles round.

She liked to see for herself and awakened the same taste in him.

Factories which, as a rule, were closed to visitors, were readily opened to the pretty elegant lady and her handsome boy, "who after all knew nothing at all about it;" and they were able to see almost all that they wished. It was a less congenial task to use her influence to turn his thoughts to higher things, but it was rarely, nevertheless, that she failed. She struggled hard over what she did not understand and sought for help. To explain these things to Rafael in the most attractive manner possible became a new occupation for her.

His natural disposition inclined him to such studies; but to a boy of thirteen, who was thus kept from his comrades and their sports, it soon became a nuisance.

No sooner had Fru Kaas noticed this than she took active steps. They left England and crossed to France.

The strange speech threw him back on her; no one shared him with her. They settled in Calais. A few days after their arrival she cut her hair short; she hoped that it would touch him to see that as he would not look like her, she tried to look like him—to be a. boy like him. She bought a smart new hat, she composed a jaunty costume, new from top to toe, for everything must be altered with the hair. But when she stood before him, looking like a girl of twenty-five, merry, almost boisterous, he was simply dismayed—nay, it was some time before he could altogether comprehend what had happened. As long as he could remember his mother, her eyes had always looked forth from beneath a crown; more solemn, more beautiful.

"Mother," he said, "where are you?"

She grew pale and grave, and stammered something about its being more comfortable—about red hair not looking well when it began to lose its colour—and went into her room. There she sat with his hair before her and her own beside it; she wept.

"Mother, where are you?" She might have answered, "Rafael, where are you?"

She went about with him everywhere. In France two handsome, stylishly dressed people are always certain to be noticed, a thing which she thoroughly appreciated.

During their different expeditions she always spoke French; he begged her to talk Norse at least now and then, but all in vain.

Here, too, they visited every possible and impossible factory. Unpractical and reserved as she was on ordinary occasions, she could be full of artifice and co-quetry whenever she wished to gain access to a steam bakery and particular as she generally was about her toilette, she would come away again sooty and grimy if thereby she could procure for Rafael some insight into mechanics. She shrank from foul air as from the cholera, yet inhaled sulphuric acid gas as though it had been ozone for his sake.

"Seeing for yourself, Rafael, is the substance, other methods are its shadow;" or "Seeing for yourself, Rafael, is meat and drink, the other is but literature."

He was not quite of the same opinion: he thought that Notre Dame de Par-is, from which he was daily dragged away, was the richest banquet that he had yet enjoyed, while from the factory of Mayel et fils there issued the most deadly odours.

His reading—she had encouraged him in it for the sake of the language and had herself helped him; now she was jealous of it and could not be persuaded to get him new books; but he got them nevertheless.

They had been in Calais for several months; he had masters and was begin-ning to feel himself at home, when there arrived at the pension a widow from one of the colonies, accompanied by her daughter, a girl of thirteen.

The new comers had not appeared at meals for more than two days before the young gentleman began to pay his court to the young lady. From the first moment it was a plain case. Very soon every one in the pension was highly amused to no-tice how fluent his French was becoming; his choice of words at times was even el-egant! The girl taught him it without a trace of grammar, by charm, sprightliness, a little nonsense; a pair of confiding eyes and a youthful voice were sufficient. It was from her that he got, by stealth, one novel after another. By stealth it had to be; by stealth Lucie had procured them; by stealth she gave them to him; by stealth they were read; by stealth she took them back again. This reading made him a little ab-sent-minded, but otherwise nothing betrayed his flights into literature: to be sure, they were not very wonderful.

Fru Kaas noticed her son's flirtation, and smiled with the rest over his prog-ress in French. She had less objection to this friendship, in which, to a great extent, she shared, than to those in England, from which she had been quite excluded. In the evenings she would take the mother and daughter out for short excursions; and these she greatly enjoyed. But the novel reading which the young people car-ried on secretly had resulted in conversations of a "grown up" type. They talked of love with the deep experience which is proper to their age, they talked with still greater discretion as to when their wedding should take place; on this point they indirectly said much which caused them many a delightful tremor. As they were accustomed to talk about themselves before others, to describe their feelings in a veiled form, it often happened when there were many people near that they carried this amusement further, and before they were themselves aware of it, they were in the full tide of a symbolic language and played "catch" with each other.

Fru Kaas noticed one evening that the word "rose" was drawn out to a greater length than it was possible for any rose to attain to; at the same time she saw the languishing look in their eyes, and broke in with the question, "What do you mean about the rose, child?"

If any one had peeped behind a rose-bush and caught them kissing one another, a thing they had never done, they could not have blushed more.

The next day Fru Kaas found new rooms, a long way from the quay near which they were living.

Rafael had suffered greatly at being torn away from England just as he had come down from his high horse and had put himself on a par with his companions, but not the least notice was taken of his trouble; it had only annoyed his mother.

To be absolutely debarred from the books he was so fond of had been hard; but up to this time, being in a foreign land, amid foreign speech, he had always fallen back upon her. Now he openly defied her. He went straight off to the hotel and sought out Madame Mery and her daughter as though nothing had occurred. This he did every day when he had finished his lessons. Lucie had now become his sole romance; he gave all his leisure time to her, and not only that (for it no longer sufficed to see her at her mother's), they met on the quay! At times a maid-servant walked with them for appearance sake, at others she kept in the background. Sometimes they would go on board a Norwegian ship, sometimes they wandered about or strolled beneath some great trees. When he saw her in her short frock come out of the door, saw her quick movements, and her lively signals to him with parasol or hat or flowers, the quay, the ships, the bales, the barrels, the air, the noise, the crowd, all seemed to play and sing,

> "Enfant! si j'etais roi je donerais l'empire,
> Et mon char, et mon septre, et mon peuple a genoux,"

and he ran to meet her.

He never dared to do more than to take both her chubby brown hands, nor to say more than "You are very sweet, you are very very good." And she never went further than to look at him, walk with him, laugh with him, and say to him, "You are not like the others." What experiences there had been in the life of this girl of thirteen goodness alone knows. He never asked her, he was too sure of her.

He learned French from her as one bird feeds from another's bill, or as one who looks at his image in a fountain, as he drinks from it.

One day, as mother and son were at breakfast, she glanced quietly across at him. "I heard of an excellent preparatory school of mechanics at Rouen," she said, "so I wrote to inquire about it, and here is the answer. I approve of it in all respects, as you will do when you read it. I think that we shall go to Rouen; what do you say to it?"

He grew first red, then white; then put down his bread, his table napkin; got up and left the room. Later in the day she asked him whether he would not read the letter; he left her without answering. At last, just as he was going to meet Lucie on the quay, she said, and this time with determination, that they were to leave in the course of an hour. She had already packed up; as they stood there the man came to fetch the luggage. At that moment he felt that he could thoroughly understand why his father had beaten her.

As they sat in the carriage which took them to the station he suffered keenly. It could not nave been worse, he thought, if his mother had stabbed him with a knife. He did not sit beside her in the railway carriage.

During the first days at Rouen he would not answer when she spoke to him, nor ask a single question. He had adopted her own tactics; he carried them through with a cruelty of which he was not aware.

For a long time he had been disposed to criticise her; now that this criticism was extended to all that she said or did, the spirit of accusation tinctured her whole life; their joint past seemed altered and debased.

His father's bent form, in the log chair on the hairless skin, malodorous and dirty, rose up before him, in vivid contrast with his mother in her well appointed, airy, perfumed rooms!

When Rafael stood by his father's body he had felt the same thing—that the old man had been badly treated. He himself had been encouraged to neglect his father, to shun him, to evade his orders. At that time he had laid the blame on the people on the estate; now he put it all down to his mother's account. His father had certainly adored her once, and this feeling had changed into wild self-consuming hatred. What had happened? He did not know; but he could not but admit that his mother would have tried the patience of Job.

He pictured to himself how Lucie would come running with her flowers, search for him over the whole quay, farther and farther every time, standing still at last. He could not think of it without tears, and without a feeling of bitterness.

But a child is a child. It was not a life-long grief. As the place was new and historically interesting, and as lessons had now begun and his mother was always with him, this feeling wore off, but the mutual restraint was still there. The critical spirit which had first been roused in England never afterwards left Rafael.

The hours of study which they passed together produced good results. Beginning as her pupil, he had ended by becoming her teacher. She was anxious to keep up with him, and this was an advantage to him, on account of her almost too minute accuracy, but still more from her intelligent questions. Apart from study they passed many pleasant hours together, but they both knew that something was missing in their conversation which could never be there again.

At longer or shorter intervals a shy silence interrupted this intercourse. Sometimes it was he, sometimes she, who, for some cause or other, often a most trivial one, elected not to reply, not to ask a question, not to see. When they were good friends he appreciated the best side of her character, the self-sacrificing life which she led for him. When they were not friends it was exactly the opposite. When they were friends, he, as a rule, did whatever she wished. He tried to atone for the past. He was in the land of courtesy and influenced by its teaching. When he was not friends with her he behaved as badly as possible. He early got among bad companions and into dissipated habits; he was the very child of Rebellion. At times he had qualms of conscience on account of it.

She guessed this, and wished him to guess that she guessed it.

"I perceive a strange atmosphere here, fie! Some one has mixed their atmosphere with yours, fie!" And she sprinkled him with scent.

He turned as red as fire and, in his shame and misery, did not know which way to look. But if he attempted to speak she became as stiff as a poker, and, raising her small hand, "Taisez-vous des egards, sil vous plait."

It must be said in her excuse that, notwithstanding the daring books which she had written, she had had no experience of real life; she knew no form of words for such an occasion. It came at last to this pass, that she, who had at one time wished to control his whole life and every thought in it, and who would not share him with any one, not even with a book, gradually became unwilling to have any relations with him outside his studies.

The French language especially lends itself to formal intercourse and diplomacy. They grasped this fact from the first. It may, indeed, have contributed to form their mutual life. It was more equitable and caused fewer collisions. At the slightest disagreement it was at once "Monsieur mon fils" or simply "Monsieur," or "Madame ma mere," or "Madame."

At one time his health seemed likely to suffer: his rapid growth and the studies, to which she kept him very closely, were too much for his strength.

But just then something remarkable occurred. At the time when Rafael was nineteen he was one day in a French chemical factory, and, as it were in a flash, saw how half the power used in the machinery might be saved. The son of the owner who had brought him there was a fellow-student. To him he confided his discovery. They worked it out together with feverish excitement to the most minute details. It was very complex, for it was the working of the factory itself which was involved. The scheme was carefully gone into by the owner, his son, and their assistants together, and it was decided to try it. It was entirely successful; LESS than half the motive power now sufficed.

Rafael was away at the time that it was inaugurated; he had gone down a mine. His mother was not with him; he never took her down mines with him. As soon as ever he returned home he hurried off with her to see the result of his work. They saw everything, and they both blushed at the respect shown to them by the workmen. They were quite touched when, the owner being called, they heard his expressions of boundless delight. Champagne flowed for them, accompanied by the warmest thanks. The mother received a beautiful bouquet. Excited by the wine and the congratulations, proud of his recognition as a genius, Rafael left the place with his mother on his arm. It seemed to him as though he were on one side, and all the rest of the world on the other. His mother walked happily beside him, with her bouquet in her hand. Rafael wore a new overcoat—one after his own heart, very long and faced with silk, and of which he was excessively proud. It was a clear winter's day; the sun shone on the silk, and on something more as well.

"There is not a speck on the sky, mother," he said.

"Nor one on your coat either," she retorted; for there had been a great many on his old one, and each had had its history.

He was too big now to be turned to ridicule, and too happy as well. She heard him humming to himself: it was the Norwegian national air. They came back to the town again as from Elysium. All the passers-by looked at them: people quickly detect happiness. Besides Rafael was a head taller than most of them and fairer in complexion. He walked quickly along beside his elegant mother, and looked across the Boulevard as though from a sunny height.

"There are days on which one feels oneself a different person," he said.

"There are days on which one receives so much," she answered, pressing his arm.

They went home, threw aside their wraps, and looked at one another. Sketches of the machinery which they had just seen lay about, as well as some rough drawings. These she collected and made into a roll.

"Rafael," she said, and drew herself up, half laughing, half trembling, "kneel; I wish to knight you."

It did not seem unnatural to him; he did so.

"Noblesse oblige," she said, and let the roll of paper approach his head; but therewith she dropped it and burst into tears.

He spent a merry evening with his friends, and was enthusiastically applauded. But as he lay in bed that night he felt utterly despondent. The whole thing might, after all, have been a mere chance. He had seen so much, had acquired so much information; it was no discovery that he had made. What was it, then? He was certainly not a genius; that must be an exaggeration. Could one imagine a genius without a victor's confidence, or had his peculiar life destroyed that confidence? This anxiety which constantly intruded itself; this bad conscience; this dreadful, vile conscience; this ineradicable dread; was it a foreboding? Did it point to the future?

It was about half a year after this that his desultory studies became concentrated on electricity, and after a time this took them to Munich. During the course of these studies he began to write, quite spontaneously. The students had formed a society, and Rafael was expected to contribute a paper. But his contribution was so original that they begged him to show it to the professor, and this encouraged him greatly. It was the professor, too, who had his first article printed. A Norwegian technical periodical accepted a subsequent one, and this was the external influence which turned his thoughts once more towards Norway. Norway rose before him as the promised land of electricity. The motive power of its countless waterfalls was sufficient for the whole world! He saw his country during the winter darkness gleaming with electric lustre. He saw her, too, the manufactory of the world, the possessor of navies. Now he had something to go home for!

His mother did not share his love for their country, and had no desire to live in Norway. But the money which she had saved up for his education bad been spent long ago. Hellebergene had had its share. The estate did not yield an equivalent, for it was essentially a timbered estate, and the trees on it were still immature.

So it was to be home! A few years alone at Hellebergene was just what he wished for. But—something always occurred to prevent their departure at the time fixed for it. First he was detained by an invention which he wished to patent. Up to the present time he had only sketched out ideas which others had adopted; now it was to be different. The invention was duly patented and handed over to an agent to sell; but still they did not start. What was the hindrance? Another invention with a fresh patent more likely to sell than the first, which unfortunately did not go off. This patent was also taken out, which again cost money, and was handed over to the agent to be sold. Could he not start now? Well, yes, he thought he could. But Fru Kaas soon realised that he was not serious, so she sought the help of a young relative, Hans Ravn, an engineer, like most of the Ravns. Rafael liked Hans, for he was himself a Ravn in temperament, a thing that he had not realised before; it was quite a revelation to him. He had believed that the Ravns were like his mother, but now found that she greatly differed from them. To Hans Ravn Fru Kaas said plainly that now they must start. The last day of May was the date fixed on, and this Hans was to tell every one, for it would make Rafael bestir himself, his mother thought, if this were known everywhere. Hans Ravn spread this news far and near, partly because it was his province to do so, partly because he hoped it would be the occasion of a farewell entertainment such as had never been seen. A banquet actually did take place amid general enthusiasm, which ended in the whole company forming a procession to escort their guest to his house. Here they encountered a crowd of officers who were proceeding home in the same manner. They nearly came to blows, but fraternised instead, and the engineers cheered the officers and the officers the engineers.

The next day the history of the two entertainments and the collision between the guests went the round of the papers.

This produced results which Fru Kaas had not foreseen. The first was a very pleasant one. The professor who had had Rafael's first article published drove up to the door, accompanied by his family. He mounted the stairs, and asked her if she would not, in their company, once more visit the prettiest parts of Munich and its vicinity. She felt flattered, and accepted the invitation. As they drove along they talked of nothing but Rafael: partly about his person, for he was the darling of every lady, partly about the future which lay before him. The professor said that he had never had a more gifted pupil. Fru Kaas had brought an excellent binocular glass with her, which she raised to her eyes from time to time to conceal her emotion, and their hearty praise seemed to flood the landscape and buildings with sunshine.

The little party lunched together, and drove home in the afternoon.

When Fru Kaas re-entered her room, she was greeted by the scent of flowers. Many of their friends who had not till now known when they were to leave had wished to pay them some compliment. Indeed, the maid said that the bell had been ringing the whole morning. A little later Rafael and Hans Ravn came in with one or two friends. They proposed to dine together. The sale of the last patent seemed to be assured, and they wished to celebrate the event. Fru Kaas was in excellent spirits, so off they went.

They dined in the open air with a number of other people round them. There was music and merriment, and the subdued hum of distant voices rose and fell in the twilight. When the lamps were lighted, they had on one side the glare of a large town, on the other the semi-darkness was only relieved by points of light; and this was made the subject of poetical allusions in speeches to the friends who were so soon to leave them.

Just then two ladies slowly passed near Rafael's chair. Fru Kaas, who was sitting opposite, noticed them, but he did not. When they had gone a short distance they stood still and waited, but did not attract his attention. Then they came slowly back again, passing close behind his chair, but still in vain. This annoyed Fru Kaas. Her individuality was so strong that her silence cast a shadow over the whole party; they broke up.

The next morning Rafael was out again on business connected with the patent. The bell rang, and the maid came in with a bill; it had been brought the previous day as well, she said. It was from one of the chief restaurateurs of the town, and was by no means a small one. Fru Kaas had no idea that Rafael owed money—least of all to a restaurateur. She told the maid to say that her son was of age, and that she was not his cashier. There was another ring—the maid reappeared with a second bill, which had also been brought the day before. It was from a well-known wine merchant; this, too, was not a small one. Another ring; this time it was a bill for flowers and by no means a trifle. This, too, had been brought the day before. Fru Kaas read it twice, three times, four times: she could not realise that Rafael owed money for flowers—what did he want them for? Another ring; now it was a bill from a jeweller. Fru Kaas became so nervous at the ringing and the bills that she took to flight. Here, then, was the explanation of their postponed departure: he was held captive; this was the reason for all his anxiety about selling the patent. He had to buy his freedom. She was hardly in the street when an unpretending little old woman stepped up to her, and asked timidly if this might be Frau von Kas? Another bill, thought Fru Kaas, eyeing her closely. She reminded one of a worn-out rose-bush with a few faded blossoms on it: she seemed poor and inexperienced in all save humility.

"What do you want with me?" inquired Fru Kaas sympathetically, resolved to pay the poor thing at once, whatever it might be.

The little woman begged "Tausend Mal um Verzeihung," but she was "Einer Beamten-Wittwe" and had read in the paper that the young Von Kas was leaving, and both she and her daughter were in such despair that she had resolved to come to Frau von Kas, who was the only one—and here she began to cry.

"What does your daughter want from me?" asked Fru Kaas rather less gently.

"Ach! tausend Mal um Verzeihung gnadige Frau," her daughter was married to Hofrath von Rathen—"ihrer grossen Schonheit wegen"—ah, she was so unhappy, for Hofrath von Rathen drank and was cruel to her. Herr von Kas had met her at the artists' fete—"Und so wissen Sie zwei so junge, reizende Leute." She looked up at Fru Kaas through her tears—looked up as though from a rain-splashed cellar window; but Fru Kaas had reverted to her abrupt manner, and as if from an upper storey the poor little woman heard, "What does your daughter want with my son?"

"Tausend Mal um Verzeihung," but it had seemed to them that her daughter might go with them to Norway, Norway was such a free country. "Und die zwei Jungen haben sich so gern."

"Has he promised her this?" said Fru Kaas, with haughty coldness.

"Nein, nein, nein," was the frightened reply. They two, mother and daughter, had thought of it that day. They had read in the paper that the young Von Kas was going away. "Herr Gott in Himmel!" if her daughter could thus be rid at once of all her troubles! Frau von Kas had not an idea of what a faithful soul, what a tender wife her daughter was.

Fru Kaas crossed hastily over to the opposite pavement. She did not go quite so fast as a person in chase of his hat, but it seemed to the poor little creature, left in the lurch, with folded hands and frightened eyes, that she had vanished faster than her hopes. On the other side of the waystood a pretty young flower-girl who was waiting for the elegant lady hurrying in her direction. "Bitte, gnadige Frau." Here is another, thought the hunted creature. She looked round for help, she flew up the street, away, away—when another lady popped up right in front of her, evidently trying to catch her eye. Fru Kaas dashed into the middle of the street and took refuge in a carriage.

"Where to?" asked the driver.

This she had not stopped to consider, but nevertheless answered boldly, "The Bavaria!"

In point of fact she had had an idea of seeing the view of the city and its environs from "Bavaria's" lofty head before leaving. There were a great many people there, but Fru Kaas's turn to go up soon came; but just as she had reached the head of the giantess and was going to look out, she heard a lady whisper close behind her, "That is his mother." It was probable that there were several mothers up there in "Bavaria's" head beside Fru Kaas, nevertheless she gathered her skirts together and hurried down again.

Rafael came home to dine with his mother; he was in the highest spirits—he had sold his patent. But he found her sitting in the farthest corner of the sofa, with her big binocular glass in her hand. When he spoke to her she did not answer, but turned the glass with the small end towards him; she wished him to look as far off as possible.

CHAPTER 3

It was a bright evening in the beginning of June that they disembarked from the steamer, and at once left the town in the boat which was to take them to Hellebergene. They did not know any of the boatmen, although they were from the estate; the boat also was new.

But the islands among which they were soon rowing were the old ones, which had long awaited them and seemed to have swum out to meet them, and now to move one behind the other so that the boat might pass between them. Neither mother nor son spoke to the men, nor did they talk to each ether. In thus keeping silence they entered into each other's feelings, for they were both awestruck. It came upon them all at once. The bright evening light over sea and islands, the aromatic fragrance from the land,—the quick splash of a little coasting steamer as she passed them—nothing could cheer them.

Their life lay there before them, bringing responsibilities both old and new. How would all that they were coming to look to them, and how far were they themselves now fitted for it?

Now they had passed the narrow entrance of the bay, and rounded the last point beneath the crags of Hellebergene. The green expanse opened out before them, the buildings in its midst. The hillsides had once been crowned and darkly clad with luxuriant woods. Now they stood there denuded, shrunk, formless, spread over with a light green growth leaving some parts bare. The lowlands, as well as the hills which framed them, were shrunk and diminished, not in extent but in appearance. They could nut persuade themselves to look at it. They recalled it all as it had been and felt themselves despoiled.

The buildings had been newly painted, but they looked small by contrast with those which they had in their minds. No one awaited them at the landing, but a few people stood about near the gallery, looking embarrassed—or were they suspicious? The travellers went into Fru Kaas's old rooms, both up stairs and down. These were just as they had left them, but how faded and wretched they looked! The table, which was laid for supper, was loaded with coarse food like that at a farmer's wedding.

The old lime-trees were gone. Fru Kaas wept.

Suddenly she was reminded of something. "Let us go across to the other wing," she said this as if there they would find what was wanting. In the gallery she took Rafael's arm; he grew curious. His father's old rooms had been entirely renovated for him. In everything, both great and small, he recognised his mother's designs and taste. A vast amount of work, unknown to him, an endless interchange of letters and a great expenditure of money. How new and bright everything looked! The rooms differed as much from what they had been, as she had endeavoured to make Rafael's life from the one that had been led in them.

They two had a comfortable meal together after all, followed by a quiet walk along the shore. The wide waters of the bay gleamed softly, and the gentle ripple took up its old story again while the summer night sank gently down upon them.

Early the next morning Rafael was out rowing in the bay, the play-ground of his childhood. Notwithstanding the shorn and sunken aspect of the hills, his delight at being there again was indescribable. Indescribable because of the loneliness and stillness: no one came to disturb him. After having lived for many years in large towns, to find oneself alone in a Norwegian bay is like leaving a noisy market-place at midday and passing into a high vaulted church where no sound penetrates from without, and where only one's own footstep breaks the silence. Holiness, purification, abstraction, devotion, but in such light and freedom as no church possesses. The lapse of time, the past were forgotten; it was as though he had never been away, as though no other place had ever known him.

Indescribable, for the intensity of his feelings surpassed anything that he had hitherto known. New sensations, impressions of beauty absolutely forgotten since childhood, or remembered but imperfectly, crowded upon him, speaking to him like welcoming spirits.

The altered contour of the hills, the dear familiar smell, the sky which seemed lower and yet farther off, the effects of light in colder tones, but paler and more delicate. Nowhere a broad plain, an endless expanse. No! all was diversified, full of contrast, broken; not lofty, still unique, fresh, he had almost said tumultuous.

Each moment he felt more in accord with his memories, his nature was in harmony with it all.

He paused between each stroke of the oars, soothed by the gentle motion; the boat glided on, he had not concerned himself whither, when he heard from behind the sound of oars which was not the echo of his own. The strokes succeeded each other at regular intervals. He turned.

At that moment Fru Kaas came out on to the terrace with her big binocular. She had had her coffee, and was ready to enjoy the view over the bay, the islands, and the open sea. Rafael, she was told, had already gone out in the boat. Yes! there he was, far out. She put up her glass at the moment that a white painted boat shot out towards his brown one. The white one was rowed by a girl in a light-coloured dress. "Grand Dieu! are there girls here too?"

Now Rafael ceases rowing, the girl does the same, they rest on their oars and the boats glide past each other. Fru Kaas could distinguish the girl's shapely neck under her dark hair, but her wide-brimmed straw hat hid her face.

Rafael lets his oars trail along the water and resting on them looks at her, and now her oars also touch the water as she turns towards him. Do they know each other? Quickly the boats draw together; Rafael puts out his hand and draws them closer, and now he gives HER his hand. Fru Kaas can see Rafael's profile so plainly that she can detect the movement of his lips. He is laughing! The stranger's face is hidden by her hat, but she can see a full figure and a vigorous arm below the half-sleeve. They do not loose their hands; now he is laughing till his broad shoulders shake. What is it? What is it? Can any one have followed him from Munich? Fru Kaas could remain where she was no longer. She went indoors and put down the glass; she was overcome by anxiety, filled with helpless anger. It was some time before she could prevail on herself to go out and resume her walk. The girl had turned her boat. Now they are rowing in side by side, she as strongly as he. Whenever Fru Kaas looked at her son he was laughing and the girl's face was turned towards his. Now they head for the landing-place at the parsonage. Was it Helene? The only girl for miles round, and Rafael had hooked himself on to her the very first day that he was at home. These girls who can never see him without taking a fancy to him! Now the boats are beached, not on the shingle, where the stones would be slippery. No! on the sand, where they have run them up as high as possible. Now she jumps lightly and quickly out of her boat, and he a little more heavily out of his; they grasp each other's hands again. Yes! there they were.

Fru Kaas turned away; she knew that for the moment she was nothing more than an old chattel pushed away into a corner.

It was Helene. She knew that they had arrived and thought that she would row past the house; and thus it was that she had encountered Rafael, who had simply gone out to amuse himself.

As they had lain on their oars and the boats glided silently past each other, he thought to himself, "That girl never grew up here, she is cast in too fine a mould for that; she is not in harmony with the place." He saw a face whose regular lines, and large grey eyes, harmonised well with each other, a quiet wise face, across which all at once there flew a roguish look. He knew it again. It had done him good before to-day. Our first thought in all recognitions, in all remembrances— that is to say, if there is occasion for it—is, has that which we recognise or recall done us good or evil?

This large mouth, those honest eyes, which have a roguish look just now, had always, done him good.

"Helene!" he cried, arresting the progress of his boat.

"Rafael!" she answered, blushing crimson and checking her boat too.

What a soft contralto voice!

When he came in to breakfast, beaming, ready to tell everything, he was confronted by two large eyes, which said as plainly as possible, "Am I put on one side already?" He became absolutely angry. During breakfast she said, in a tone of indifference, that she was going to drive to the Dean's, to thank him for the supervision which he had given to the estate during all these years. He did not answer, from which she inferred that he did not wish to go with her. It was some time before she started. The harness was new, the stable-boy raw and untrained. She saw nothing more of Rafael.

She was received at the parsonage with the greatest respect, and yet very heartily. The Dean was a fine old man and thoroughly practical. His wife was of profounder nature. Both protested that the care of the estate had been no trouble to them, it had only been a pleasant employment; Helene had now undertaken it.

"Helene?"

Yes; it had so chanced that the first bailiff at Hellebergene had once been agronomist and forester on a large concern which was in liquidation, Helene had taken such a fancy to him, that when she was not at school, she went with him everywhere; and, indeed, he was a wonderful old man. During these rambles she had learned all that he could teach her. He had an especial gift for forestry. It was a development for her, for it gave a fresh interest to her life. Little by little she had taken over the whole care of the estate. It absorbed her.

Fru Kaas asked if she might see Helene, to thank her.

"But Helene has just gone out with Rafael, has she not?"

"Yes, to be sure," answered Fru Kaas. She would not show surprise; but she asked at once for her carriage.

Meanwhile the two young people had determined to climb the ridge. At first they followed the course of the river, Helene leading the way. It was evident that she had grown up in the woods. How strong and supple she was, and how well she acquitted herself when she had to cross a brook, climb a wooded slope, force a way through a barrier of bristly young fir-trees which opposed her passage, or surmount a heap of clay at a quarry, of which there were a great many about there. Each difficulty was in turn overcome. The ascent from the river was the most direct and the pleasantest, which was the reason that they had come this way. Rafael would not be outdone by her, and kept close at her heels. But, great heavens! what it cost him. Partly because he was out of practice, partly —

"It is a little difficult to get over here," she said. A tree had fallen during the last rainy weather, and hung half suspended by its roots, obstructing the path. "You must not hold by it, it might give way and drag us with it."

At last there is something which she considers difficult, he thought.

She deliberated for a moment before the farthest-spreading branches which had to be crossed; then, lifting her skirts to her knees, over them she went, and over the next ones as well, and then across the trunk to the farthest side, where there were no branches in the way; then obliquely up the hillside. She stood still at the top of the height and watched him crawl up after her.

It cost him a struggle; he was out of breath and the perspiration poured off him. When he got up to her, everything swam before him; and although it was only for a fraction of a second, it left him fairly captivated by her strength.

She stood and looked at him with bright, roguish eyes. She was flushed and hot, and her bosom rose and fell quickly; but there was no doubt that she could at once have taken an equally long and steep climb. He was not able to speak a word.

"Now turn round and look at the sea," she said.

The words affected him as though great Pan had uttered them from the mountains far behind. He turned his eyes towards them. It seemed as though Nature herself had spoken to him. The words caressed him as with a hand now cold, now warm, and he became a different being. For he had lost himself—lost himself in her as she walked along the river-bank and climbed the hillside. She seemed to draw fresh power from the woods, to grow taller, more agile, more vigorous. The fervour of her eyes, the richness of her voice, the grace of her movements, the glimpses of her soul, had allured him down there in the valley, beside the rushing river, and the feeling of loss of individuality had increased with the exertion and the excitement. No ball-room or play-ground, no gymnasium or riding-school can display the physical powers, and the spirit which underlies them, the unity of mind and body, as does the scaling of steep hills and rocky slopes. At last, intoxicated by these feelings, he thought to himself—I am climbing after her, climbing to the highest pinnacle of happiness. Up there! Up there! The composure of her manner towards him, her freedom from embarrassment, maddened him. Up there! Up there! And ever as they mounted she became more spirited, he more distressed. Up there! Up there! His eyes grew dim, for a few seconds he could not move, could not speak. Then she had said, "Now you must look at the sea."

He seemed to see with different eyes, to be endowed with new sensations, and these new sensations gave answer to what the distant mountains had said. They answered the sea out there before him, the island-studded sea, the open sea beyond, the wide swelling ocean, the desires and destinies of life all the world over. The sea lay steel-bright beneath the suffused sunlight, and seemed to gaze on the rugged land as on a beloved child instinct with vital power. Cling thou to the mighty one, or thy strength will be thine undoing!

And many of the inventions which he had dreamed of loomed vaguely before him. They lay outside there. It depended on him whether he should one day bring them safely into port.

"What are you thinking about?" said she, the sound of her voice put these thoughts to flight and recalled him to the present. He felt how full and rich her contralto voice was, A moment ago he could have told her this, and more besides, as an introduction to still more. Now he sat down without answering, and she did the same.

"I come up here very often," she said, "to look at the sea. From here it seems the source of life and death; down there it is a mere highway." He smiled. She continued: "The sea has this power, that whatever pre-occupation one may bring up here, it vanishes in a moment; but down below it remains with one."

He looked at her.

"Yes, it is true," said she, and coloured.

"I do not in the least doubt it," he replied.

But she did not continue the subject. "You are looking at the saplings, I see."

"Yes."

"You must know that last year there was a long drought; almost all the young trees up here withered away, and in other places on the hillsides also, as you see." She pointed as she spoke. "It looks so ugly as one comes into the bay. I thought about that yesterday. I thought also that you should not be here long before you saw that you had done us an injustice, for could anything be prettier than that little fir-tree down there in the hollow? just look at its colour; that is a healthy fellow! and these sturdy saplings, and that little gem there!" The tones of Helene's voice betrayed the interest which she felt. "But how that one over there has grown." She scrambled across to it, and he after her. "Do you see? two branches already; and what branches!" They knelt down beside it. "This boy has had parents of whom he can boast, for they have all had just as much and just as little shelter. Oh! the disgusting caterpillars." She was down before the little tree at the side which was being spun over. She cleared it, and got up to fetch some wet mould, which she laid carefully round the sprouts. "Poor thing I it wants water, although it rained tremendously a little time ago."

"Are you often up here?" he asked.

"It would all come to nothing if I were not!" She looked at him searchingly. "You do not, perhaps, believe that this little tree knows me; every one of them, indeed. If I am long away from them they do not thrive, but when I am often with them they flourish." She was on her knees, supporting herself with one hand, while with the other she pulled up some grass. "The thieves," said she, "which want to rob my saplings."

If it had been a little person who had said this; a little person with lively eyes and a merry mouth—but Helene was tall and stately; her eyes were not lively, but met one with a steady gaze. Her mouth was large, and gave deliberate utterance to her thoughts.

Whoever has read Helene's words quickly, hurriedly, must read them over again. She spoke quietly and thoughtfully, each syllable distinct and musical. She was not the same girl who had led the way by river and hill. Then she seemed to glory in her strength; now her energy had changed to delicate feeling.

One of the most remarkable women in Scandinavia, who also had these two sides to her character, and made the fullest use of both, Johanne Luise Hejberg, once saw Helene when she had but just attained to womanhood. She could not take her eyes off her; she never tired of watching her and listening to her. Did the aged woman, then at the close of her life, recognise anything of her own youth in the girl? Outwardly too they resembled each other. Helene was dark, as Fru Hejberg had been; was about the same height, with the same figure, but stronger; had a large mouth, large grey eyes like hers, into which the same roguish look would start. But the greatest likeness was to be found in their natures: in Fru Hejberg's expression when she was quiet and serious; in a certain motherliness which was the salient feature in her nature.

"What a healthy girl!" said she; bade some one bring Helene to her, and drawing her towards her, kissed her on the forehead.

Helene and her companion had crossed to the other side of the hill, for he positively must see the "Buckthorn Swamp"; but when they got down there he did not know it again: it was covered by luxuriant woods.

"Yes! It is old Helgesen who deserves the credit of that," she said. "He noticed that an artificial embankment had converted this great flat into a swamp, so he cut through it. I was only a child then, but I had my share in it. They gave me a bit of ground down by the river to plant Kohl Kabi in. I looked after it the whole summer. Later on I had a larger piece. With the profits we cut ditches up to here. In the fourth year we bought plants. In fact, he so arranged it, that I paid for it all with my work, the old rogue!"

When Rafael got home his mother was at table: she had not waited for him, a sure sign that she felt aggrieved. No attempts on his part to set things right succeeded. She would not answer, and soon left the room. It now struck him how pleasant it would have been for his mother if he had taken her with him to explore and make acquaintance with this new Hellebergene. The evening before, in his father's rooms, it had seemed as though nothing could ever separate them—and the first thing in the morning he was off with some one else. This evening he knew that nothing could be done, but next morning he begged her earnestly to come with them, and they would show her what he had seen the day before; but she only shook her head and took up a book. Day after day he made a similar request, but always with the same result. She thought that these invitations were merely formal, and so, from one point of view, they were. He was most ready to appease her, most ready to show her everything, for he felt himself to blame, though he certainly thought that she might have understood; but her presence would have marred their tete-a-tete; he would have been embarrassed enough if she had acquiesced!

The Dean, with his wife and daughter, came the following Sunday to return Fru Kaas's visit. She was politeness itself, and specially thanked Helene for her care of Hellebergene. Helene coloured without knowing why, but when Rafael also coloured, she blushed still deeper. This was the event of the visit; nothing else of importance occurred.

In their daily walks through the fields and woods, the two young people soon exhausted the topic of Hellebergene. He took up another theme. His inventions became the topic of conversation. He had acquired, from his studies with his mother, an unusual facility in explaining his meaning, and in Helene he found a listener such as he had rarely before met with. She was sufficiently acquainted with the laws of nature to understand a simple description. But all the same it was not his inventions but himself that he discoursed on. He quite realised this, and became all the more eager. Her eyes made his reasoning clearer. He had never before had such complete faith in himself as when near her, and now no misgivings succeeded.

Helene, however, had not hitherto known the direction and results of his studies. He was an engineer, that was all that she had heard on the subject. When he had told her more about it he rose considerably in her estimation. It was SHE now who began to feel constrained. At first she did not understand why she felt obliged to put more restraint upon herself. After a time she began to excuse herself from joining him, and their walks became more rare. "She had so much to do now."

He did not comprehend the reason of this; he fancied that his mother might be to blame (which, by the way, was quite a mistake), and he grew angry. He was already greatly affronted that his mother had chosen to confound his former gallantries with his present attachment. He quite forgot that at first he had merely sought to amuse himself here as elsewhere. He gave himself up entirely to his passion, which would brook no hindrance, no opposition; it became majestic. In Helene he had found his future life.

But her parents had grown less cordial of late owing to Fru Kaas's coldness, and the time came when all attempts to obtain meetings with Helene failed. He had never been so infatuated. He seemed to see her continually before him—her luxuriant beauty, her light step, her grey eyes gazing steadfastly into his.

Why could they not be married to-morrow or the next day? What could be more natural? What could more certainly help him forward?

The constraint between his mother and himself had reached a greater pitch than ever before. He thought seriously of leaving her and the country. He still had some money left, the proceeds of the patent, and he could easily make more. How irksome it became to him to go into the fields and woods without Helene! He could not study; he had no one to talk to; what should he do?

Devote himself to boating!—row out far beyond the bay, right up to the town! One day, as he rowed along the coast, beyond the bay, he noticed that the clay and flag-stone formation in the hills and ridges was speckled with grey. Helene had told him how extraordinary it looked out there now that the trees were gone, but as they would have had to come out in the boat to see it he had let the remark pass. Now he decided to land there. The shore rose steeply from the water, but he scrambled up. He had expected to find limestone, but he could hardly believe his own eyes: it was cement stone! Absolutely, undoubtedly, cement stone! How far did it extend? As far as he could see; it might even extend to the boundary of the estate. In any case, here was sufficient for extensive works for many, many years, if only there were enough silica with the clay and lime. He had soon knocked off a few pieces, which he put into the boat, and set out for home to analyse them.

Seldom had any one rowed faster than he did; now he shot past the islands into the bay, up to the landing-place before the house. If the cement stone contained the right proportions, here was what would make Helene and himself independent of every one; AND THAT AT ONCE!

A little later, with dirty hands and clothes, his face bathed in perspiration, he rushed up to his mother with the result of his investigations.

"Here is something for you to see."

She was reading; she looked up and turned as white as a sheet.

"Is that the cement stone?" she asked, as she put down her book.

"Did you know about it?" he exclaimed, in the greatest astonishment.

"Good gracious, yes," she answered. She walked across to the window, came back again, pressing her hands together. "So you have found it too?"

"Who did before me?"

"Your father, Rafael, your father, the first time that I was here, a little time before we were to leave." She paused. "He came rushing in as you did just now—not so quickly, not so quickly, he was weak in the legs, but otherwise just like you." She let her eyes rest, with a peculiar look, on Rafael's dirty hands. The hands themselves were not well shaped, they were almost exactly his father's.

Rafael noticed nothing.

"Had HE found the bed of cement stone, then?"

"Yes. He locked the door behind him. I got up from my chair and asked him how he dared? He could hardly speak." She paused for a moment, recalling it all again. "Yes, and it was THAT stuff."

"What did he say, mother?"

She had turned to leave the room.

"Your father believed that I had brought luck to the house."

"And why was it not so, then?"

She faced him quickly. He coloured.

"Pardon, mother, you misunderstood me. I meant, why did it come to nothing about the cement?"

"You did not know your father: there were too many hooks about him for him to be able to carry out anything."

"Hooks?"

"Yes! eccentricity, egotism, passion, which caught fast in everything."

"What did he propose to do?"

"No one was to be allowed to have anything to do with it, no one was to know of it, he was to be everything! For this reason the timber was to be cut down and sold; and when we were married—I say when we were married, the whole of my fortune was to be used as well."

He saw the horror with which she still regarded it; she was passing through the whole struggle again; and he understood that he must not question her further. She made a gesture with her hand; and he asked hurriedly, "Why did you not tell me before, mother?"

"Because it would have brought you no good," she answered decidedly.

He felt, nay, he saw that she believed that it would bring him no good now. She again raised her hand, and he left her.

When he was once more in the boat, taking his great news to the parsonage, he thought to himself, Here is the reason of my father's and mother's deadly enmity.

The cement stone! She did not trust him, she would not give him both herself and her fortune, so there was no cement, nor were any trees felled.

"Well, he scored after all. Yes, and mother too; but God help ME!"

Then he reckoned up what the timber and the fortune together would have been worth, and what further sum could have been raised on the property, the value of the cement-bed being taken into consideration. He understood his father better than his mother. What a fortune, what power, what magnificence, what a life!

At the parsonage he carried every one with him.

The Dean, because he saw at once what this was worth. "You are a rich man now," he said. The Dean's wife, because she felt attracted by his ability and enthusiasm. Helene? Helene was silent and frightened. He turned towards her and asked if she would come with him in the boat to see it. She really must see how extensive the bed was.

"Yes, dear, go with him," said her father.

Rafael wished to sit behind her in the boat and hastened towards the bow; but, without a word, she passed him, sat down, and took her oars; so, after all, he had to sit in front of her.

They thus began at cross purposes. His back was towards her, he saw how the water foamed under her oars, there was a secret struggle, a tacit fear, which was heard in the few words which they exchanged, and which merely increased their constraint.

When they drew near to their destination they were flushed and hot. Now he was obliged to turn round to look for the place of landing. To begin with, they went slowly along the whole cement-bed as far as it was visible. He was now turned so as to face her, and he explained it all to her. She kept her eyes fixed on the cliff, and only glanced at him, or did not look at him all. They turned the boat again, in order to land at the place where he intended the factory to stand. A portion of the rock would have to be blasted to make room, the harbour too must be made safer so that vessels might lie close in, and all this would cost money.

He landed first in order to help her, but she jumped on shore without his assistance; then they climbed upwards, he leading the way, explaining everything as he went; she following with eyes and ears intent.

All for which, from her childhood, she had worked so hard at Hellebergene, and all which she had dreamed of for the estate, had become so little now. It would be many years before the trees yielded any return. But here was promise of immediate prosperity and future wealth if, as she never doubted, he proved to be correct. She felt that this humbled her, made her of no account, but ah! how great it made him seem!

The rowing, the climbing, the excitement, gave animation to Rafael's explanations; face and figure showed his state of tension. She felt almost giddy: should she return to the boat and row away alone? But she was too proud thus to betray herself.

It seemed to her that there was the look of a conqueror in his eyes; but she did not intend to be conquered. Neither did she wish to appear as the one who had remained at home and speculated on his return. That would be simply to turn all that was most cherished, most unselfish in her life, against herself. Something in him frightened her, something which, perhaps, he himself could not master—his inward agitation. It was not boisterous or terrifying; it was glowing, earnest zeal, which seemed to deprive him of power and her of will, and this she would not endure.

Hardly had they gained the summit from which they could look out over the islands to the open sea, and across to Hellebergene, to the parsonage, and the river flowing into the inner bay, than he turned away from it all towards her, as she stood with heaving breast, glowing cheeks, and eyes which dare not turn away from the sea.

"Helene," he whispered, approaching her; he wished to take her in his arms.

She trembled, although she did not turn round; the next moment she sprang away from him, and did not pause till she had got down to the boat, which she was about to push off, but bethought herself that it would be too cowardly, so she remained standing and watched him come after her.

"Helene," he called from above, "why do you run away from me?"

"Rafael, you must not," she answered when he rejoined her. The strongest accent of both prayer and command of which a powerful nature is capable sounded in her words. She in the boat, he on the shore; they eyed one another like two antagonists, watchful and breathing hard, till he loosed the boat, stepped in and pushed off.

She took her seat; but before doing the same he said:

"You know quite well what I wanted to say to you." He spoke with difficulty.

She did not answer and got out her oars; her tears were ready to flow. They rowed home again more slowly than they had come.

A lark hovered over their heads. The note of a thrush was heard away inland. A guillemot skimmed over the water in the same direction as their own, and a tern on curved wing screamed in their wake. There was a sense of expectation over all. The scent of the young fir-trees and the heather was wafted out to them; farther in lay the flowery meadows of Hellebergene. At a great distance an eagle could be seen, high in air, winging his way from the mountains, followed by a flock of screaming crows, who imagined that they were chasing him. Rafael drew Helene's attention to them.

"Yes, look at them," she said; and these few words, spoken naturally, helped to put both more at their ease. He looked round at her and smiled, and she smiled back at him. He felt in the seventh heaven of delight, but it must not be spoken. But the oars seemed to repeat in measured cadence, "It—is—she. It—is—she. It—is—she." He said to himself, Is not her resistance a thousand times sweeter than—

"It is strange that the sea birds no longer breed on the islands in here," he said.

"That is because for a long time the birds have not been protected; they have gone farther out."

"They must be protected again: we must manage to bring the birds back, must we not?"

"Yes," she answered.

He turned quickly towards her. Perhaps she should not have said that, she thought, for had he not said "we"?

To show how far she was from such a thought, she looked towards the land. "The clover is not good this year."

"No. What shall you do with the plot next year?"

But she did not fall into the trap. He turned round, but she looked away.

Now the rush of the river tossed them up and down in a giddy dance, as the force of the stream met the boat. Rafael looked up to where they had walked together the first day. He turned to see if she were not, by chance, looking in the same direction. Yes, she was!

They rowed on towards the landing-place at the parsonage, and he spoke once or twice, but she had learned that that was dangerous. They reached the beach.

"Helene!" said he, as she jumped on shore with a good-bye in passing, "Helene!" But she did not stay. "Helene!" he shouted, with such meaning in it that she turned.

She looked at him, but only remained for a moment. No more was needed! He rowed home like the greatest conqueror that those waters had ever seen. Ever since the Vikings had met together in the innermost creek, and left behind them the barrow which is still to be seen near the parsonage—yes, ever since the elk of the primaeval forest, with mighty antlers, swam away from the doe which he had won in combat, to the other which he heard on the opposite shore. Since the first swarm of ants, like a waving fan, danced up and down in the sunlight, on its one day of flight. Since the first seals struggled against each other to reach the one whom they saw lie sunning herself on the rocks.

Fru Kaas had seen them pass as they rowed out at a furious pace. She had seen them row slowly back, and she understood everything. No sooner had the cement stone been found than—

She paced up and down; she wept.

She did not put any dependence on his constancy; in any case it was too early for Rafael to settle himself here: he had something very different before him. The cement stone would not run away from him, or the girl either, if there were anything serious in it. She regarded his meeting with Helene as merely an obstacle in the way, which barred his further progress.

Rafael rowed towards home, bending to his oars till the water foamed under the bow of his boat. Now he has landed; now he drags the boat up as if she were an eel-pot. Now he strides quickly up to the house.

Frightened, despairing, his mother shrank into the farthest corner of the sofa, with her feet drawn up under her, and, as he burst in through the door and began to speak, she cried out: "Taisez-vous! des egards, s'il vous plait." She stretched out her arms before her as if for protection. But now he came, borne on the wings of love and happiness. His future was there.

He did what he had never done before: went straight up to her, drew her arms down, embraced and kissed her, first on the forehead, then on the cheeks, eyes, mouth, ears, neck, wherever he could; all without a word.

He was quite beside himself.

"Mad boy," she gasped; "des egards, mais Rafael, donc!—Que—" And she threw herself on his breast with her arms round his neck.

"Now you will forsake me, Rafael," she said, crying.

"Forsake you, mother! No one can unite the two wings like Helene."

And now he began a panegyric on her, without measure, and unconscious that he said the same thing over and over again. When he became quieter, and she was permitted to breathe, she begged to be alone: she was used to being alone. In the evening she came down to him, and said that, first of all, they ought to go to Christiania, and find an expert to examine the cement-bed and learn what further should be done. Her cousin, the Government Secretary, would be able to advise them, and some of her other relations as well. Most of them were engineers and men of business. He was reluctant to leave Hellebergene just now, he said, she must understand that; besides, they had agreed not to go away until the autumn. But she maintained that this was the surest way to win Helene; only she begged that, with regard to her, things should remain as they were till they had been to Christiania. On this point she was inflexible, and it was so arranged.

As was their custom, they packed up at once. They drove over to the parsonage that same evening to say good-bye. They were all very merry there: on Fru Kaas's side because she was uneasy, and wished to conceal the fact by an appearance of liveliness; on the Dean's part because he really was in high spirits at the discovery which promised prosperity both to Hellebergene and the district; on his wife's because she suspected something. The most hearty good wishes were therefore expressed for their journey.

Rafael had availed himself of the general preoccupation to exchange a few last words with Helene in a corner. He obtained a half-promise from her that when he wrote she would answer; but he was careful not to say that he had spoken to his mother. He felt that Helene would be startled by a proceeding which came quite naturally to him.

As they drove away, he waved his hat as long as they remained in sight. The waving was returned, first by all, but finally by only one.

The summer evening was light and warm, but not light enough, not warm enough, not wide enough; there did not seem room enough in it for him; it was not bright enough to reflect his happiness. He could not sleep, yet he did not wish to talk; companionship or solitude were alike distasteful to him. He thought seriously of walking or rowing over to the parsonage again and knocking at the window of Helene's room. He actually went down to the boathouse and got out the boat. But perhaps it would frighten her, and possibly injure his own cause. So he rowed out and out to the farthest islands, and there he frightened the birds. At his approach they rose: first a few, then many, then all protested in a hideous chorus of wild screams. He was enveloped in an angry crowd, a pandemonium of birds. But it did not ruffle his good humour. "Wait a bit," he said to them. "Wait a bit, until the islands at Hellebergene are 'protected,' and the whole estate as well. Then you shall come and be happy with us. Good-bye till then!"

CHAPTER 4

He came to Christiania like a tall ship gay with flags. His love was the music on board.

His numerous relations were ready to receive him. Of these many were engineers, who were a jour with all his writings, which they had taken care should be well known. Some of the largest mechanical undertakings in the country were in their hands, so that they had connections in every direction.

Once more the family had a genius in its midst; that is to say, one to make a show with. Rafael went from entertainment to entertainment, from presentation to presentation, and wherever he or his mother went court was paid to them.

In all this the ladies of the family were even more active than their lords; and they had not been in the town many days before every one knew that they were to be the rage.

There are some people who always will hold aloof. They are as irresponsive as a sooty kettle when you strike it. They are like peevish children who say "I won't," or surly old dogs who growl at every one. But HE was so exceedingly genial, a capital fellow with the highest spirits. He had looks as well; he was six feet high; and all those six feet were clothed in perfect taste. He had large flashing eyes and a broad forehead. He was practised in making clear to others all in which he was interested, and at such times how handsome he looked! He was a thorough man of the world, able to converse in several languages at the cosmopolitan dinners which were a speciality of the Ravns. He was the owner of one of the few extensive estates in Norway, and had the control, it was said, of a considerable fortune besides.

The half of this would have been enough to set all tongues wagging; therefore, first the family, then their friends, then the whole town feted him. He was a nine days' wonder! One must know the critical, unimaginative natives of Christiania, who daily pick each other to pieces to fill the void in their existences; one must have admired their endless worrying of threadbare topics to understand what it must be when they got hold of a fresh theme.

Nothing which flies before the storm is more dangerous than desert sand, nothing can surpass a Christiania FUROR.

When it became known that two of his relations who were conversant with the subject, together with a distinguished geologist and a superintendent of mines, had been down to Hellebergene with Rafael, and had found that his statements were well grounded, he was captured and borne off in triumph twenty times a day. It was trying work, but HE was always in the vein, and ready to take the rough with the smooth. In all respects the young madcap was up to the standard, so that day and night passed in a ceaseless whirl, which left every one but himself breathless. The glorious month at Hellebergene had done good. He was drawn into endless jovial adventures, so strange, so audacious, that one would have staked one's existence that such things were impossible in Christiania. But great dryness begets thirst. He was in the humour of a boy who has got possession of a jam-pot, whose mouth, nose, and hands are all besmirched. It is thus that ladies like children best; then they are the sweetest things in the world.

Like a tall, full-grown mountain-ash covered by a flock of starlings, he was the centre of a fluttering crowd. It only remained for him to be deified, and this too came to pass. One day he visited several factories, giving a hint here, another there (he had great practical knowledge and a quick eye) and every hint was of value.

At last in a factory of something the same description as the one in France where he had been the means of economising half the motive power, he suggested a similar plan; he saw on the spot how it could be effected. This became the subject of much conversation. It grew and grew, it rose like the sea after days of westerly gales. This new genius, but little over twenty, would surely some day be the wonder of the country. It soon became the fashion for every manufacturer to invite him to visit his factory, and it was only after they were convinced that they had a god among them that it became serious, for enthusiasm in a manufacturer strikes every one. The ladies only waited for this important moment to go at a bound from the lowest degree of sense to the fifth degree of madness. Their eyes danced on him like sunlight on polished metal. He himself paid little heed to degree or temperature; he was too happy in his genial contentment, and too indifferent as well. One thing which greatly helped to bring him to the right pitch was the family temperament, for it was so like his own. He was a Ravn through and through, with perhaps a little grain of Kaas added. He was what they called pure Ravn, quite unalloyed. He seemed to them to have come straight from the fountain-head of their race, endowed with its primitive strength. This strong physical attribute had perhaps made his abilities more fertile, but the family claimed the abilities, too, as their own.

Through Hans Ravn, Rafael had learned to value the companionship of his relations; now he had it in perfection. For every word that he said appreciative laughter was ready—it really sparkled round him. When he disagreed with prevailing tastes, prejudices, and morals, they disagreed too. When his precocious intelligence burst upon them, they were always ready to applaud. They even met him half-way—they could foresee the direction of his thoughts. As he was young in years and disposition, and at the same time knew more than most young people, he suited both old and young. Ah! how he prospered in Norway!

His mother went with him everywhere. Her life had at one time appeared to her relations to be most objectless, but how much she had made of it! They respected her persevering efforts to attain the goal, and she became aware of this. In the most elegant toilettes, with her discreet manner and distinguished deportment, she was hurried from party to party, from excursion to excursion, until it became too much for her.

It went too far, too; her taste was offended by it; she grew frightened. But the train of dissipation went on without her, like a string of carriages which bore him along with it while she was shaken off. Her eyes followed the cloud of dust far away, and the roll of the wheels echoed back to her.

Helene—how about Helene? Was she too out in the cold? Far from it. Rafael was as certain that she was with him as that his gold watch was next his heart. The very first day that he arrived he wrote a letter to her. It was not long, he had not time for that, but it was thoroughly characteristic. He received an answer at once; the hostess of the pension brought it to him herself. He was so immensely delighted that the lady, who was related to the Dean and who had noticed the post mark, divined the whole affair—a thing which amused him greatly.

But Helene's letter was evasive; she evidently knew him too little to dare to speak out.

He never found time to draw the hostess into conversation on the subject, however. He came home late, he got up late, and then there were always friends waiting for him; so that he was not seen in the pension again until he returned to dress for dinner, during which time the carriage waited at the door, for he never got home till the last moment.

When could he write? It would soon all be done with, and then home to Helene!

The business respecting the cement detained him longer than he had anticipated. His mother made complications; not that she opposed the formation of a company, but she raised many difficulties: she should certainly prefer to have the whole affair postponed. He had no time to talk her round, besides, she irritated him. He told it to the hostess.

A curious being, this hostess, who directed the pension, the business of the inmates, and a number of children, without apparent effort. She was a widow; two of her children were nearly twenty, but she looked scarcely thirty. Tall, dark, clever, with eyes like glowing coals; decided, ready in conversation as in business, like an officer long used to command, always trusted, always obeyed; one yielded oneself involuntarily to her matter-of-course way of arranging everything, and she was obliging, even self-sacrificing, to those she liked—it was true that that was not everybody. This absence of reserve was especially characteristic of her, and was another reason why all relied on her. She had long ago taken up Fru Kaas— entertained her first and foremost. Angelika Nagel used in conversation modern Christiania slang which is the latest development of the language. In the choice of expressions, words such as hideous were applied to what was the very opposite of hideous, such as "hideously amusing," "hideously handsome." "Snapping" to anything that was liquid, as "snapping good punch." One did not say "PRETTY" but "quite too pretty" or "hugely pretty." On the other hand, one did not say "bad" for anything serious, but with comical moderation "baddish." Anything that there was much of went by miles; for instance, "miles of virtue." This slipshod style of talk, which the idlers of large towns affect, had just become the fashion in

Christiania. All this seemed new and characteristic to the careless emancipated party which had arisen as a protest against the prudery which Fru Kaas, in her time, had combated. The type therefore amused her:—she studied it.

Angelika Nagel relieved her of all her business cares, which were only play to her. It was the same thing with the question of the cement undertaking. In an apparently careless manner she let drop what had been said and done about it, which had its effect on Fru Kaas. Soon things had progressed so far that it became necessary to consult Rafael about it, and as he was difficult to catch, she sat up for him at night. The first time that she opened the door for him he was absolutely shy, and when he heard what she wanted him for he was above measure grateful. The next time he kissed her! She laughed and ran away without speaking to him—that was all he got for his pains. But he had held her in his arms, and he glowed with a suddenly awakened passion.

She, in the meantime, kept out of his way, even during the day he never saw her unless he sought her. But when he least expected it she again met him at the door; there was something which she really MUST say to him. There was a struggle, but at last she twisted herself away from him and disappeared. He whispered after her as loud as he dared, "Then I shall go away!"

But while he was undressing she slipped into his room.

The next day, before he was quite awake, the postman brought him the warrant for a post-office order for fifteen thousand francs. He thought that there must be a mistake in the name, or else that it was a commission that had been entrusted to him. No! it was from the French manufacturer whose working expenses he had reduced so greatly. He permitted himself, he wrote, to send this as a modest honorarium. He had not been able to do so sooner, but now hoped that it would not end there. He awaited Rafael's acknowledgment with great anxiety, as he was not sure of his address.

Rafael was up and dressed in a trice. He told his news to every one, ran down to his mother and up again; but he had not been a moment alone before the superabundance of happiness and sense of victory frightened him. Now there must be an end of all this, now he would go home. He had not had the slightest prickings of conscience, the slightest longings, until now; all at once they were uncontrollable. SHE stood upon the hilltop, pure and noble. It became agonising. He must go at once, or it would drive him mad. This anxiety was made less acute by the sight of his mother's sincere pleasure. She came up to him when she heard that he had shut himself into his room. They had a really comfortable talk together—finally about the state of their finances. They lived in the pension because they could no longer afford to live in an hotel. The estate would bring nothing in until the timber once more became profitable, and her capital was no longer intact—notwithstanding the prohibition. Now she was ready to let him arrange about the cement company. On this he went out into the town, where his court soon gathered round him.

But the large sum of money which was required could not be raised in a day, so the affair dragged on. He grew impatient, he must and would go; and finally his mother induced her cousin, the Government Secretary, to form the company, and they prepared to leave. They paid farewell visits to some of their friends, and sent cards and messages of thanks to the rest. Everything was ready, the very day had come, when Rafael, before he was up, received a letter from the Dean.

An anonymous letter from Christiania, he wrote, had drawn his attention to Rafael's manner of life there, and he had in consequence obtained further information, the result being that he was, that day, sending his daughter abroad. There was nothing more in the letter. But Rafael could guess what had passed between father and daughter.

He dressed himself and rushed down to his mother. His indignation against the rascally creatures who had ruined his and Helene's future—"Who could it have been?"—was equalled by his despair. She was the only one he cared for; all the others might go to the deuce. He felt angry, too, that the Dean, or any one else, should have dared to treat him in this way, to dismiss him like a servant, not to speak to him, not to put him in a position to speak for himself.

His mother had read the letter calmly, and now she listened to him calmly, and when he became still more furious she burst out laughing. It was not their habit to settle their differences by words; but this time it flashed into his mind that she had not persuaded him to come here merely on account of the cement, but in order to separate him from Helene, and this he said to her.

"Yes," he added, "now it will be just the same with me as it was with my father, and it will be your fault this time as well." With this he went out.

Fru Kaas left Christiania shortly afterwards, and he left the same evening—for France.

From France he wrote the most pressing letter to the Dean, begging him to allow Helene to return home, so that they could be married at once. Whatever the Dean had heard about his life in Christiania had nothing to do with the feelings which he nourished for Helene. She, and she alone, had the power to bind him; he would remain hers for life.

The Dean did not answer him.

A month later he wrote again, acknowledging this time that he had behaved foolishly. He had been merely thoughtless. He had been led on by other things. The details were deceptive, but he swore that this should be the end of it all. He would show that he deserved to be trusted; nay, he HAD shown it ever since he left Christiania. He begged the Dean to be magnanimous. This was practically exile for him, for he could not return to Hellebergene without Helene. Everything which he loved there had become consecrated by her presence; every project which he had formed they had planned together; in fact, his whole future—He fretted and pined till he found it impossible to work as seriously as he wished to do.

This time he received an answer—a brief one.

The Dean wrote that only a lengthened probation could convince them of the sincerity of his purpose.

So it was not to be home, then, and not work; at all events, not work of any value. He knew his mother too well to doubt that now the cement business was shelved, whether the company were formed or not—he was only too sure of that.

He had written to his mother, begging earnestly to be forgiven for what he had said. She must know that it was only the heat of the moment. She must know how fond he was of her, and how unhappy he felt at being in discord with her on the subject which was, and always would be, most dear to him.

She answered him prettily and at some length, without a word about what had happened or about Helene. She gave him a great deal of news, among other things what the Dean intended to do about the estate.

From this he concluded that she was on the same terms with the Dean as before. Perhaps his latest reasons for deferring the affair was precisely this: that he saw that Fru Kaas did not interest herself for it.

It wore on towards the autumn. All this uncertainty made him feel lonely, and his thoughts turned towards his friends at Christiania. He wrote to tell them that he intended to make towards home. He meant, however, to remain a little time at Copenhagen.

At Copenhagen he met Angelika Nagel again. She was in company with two of his student friends. She was in the highest spirits, glowing with health and beauty, and with that jaunty assurance which turns the heads of young men.

He had, during all this time, banished the subject of his intrigue from his mind, and he came there without the least intention of renewing it; but now, for the first time in his life, he became jealous!

It was quite a novel feeling, and he was not prepared to resist it. He grew jealous if he so much as saw her in company with either of the young men. She had a hearty outspoken manner, which rekindled his former passion.

Now a new phase of his life began, divided between furious jealousy and passionate devotion. This led, after her departure, to an interchange of letters, which ended in his following her to Christiania.

On board the steamer he overheard a conversation between the steward and stewardess. "She sat up for him of nights till she got what she wanted, and now she has got hold of him."

It was possible that this conversation did not concern him, but it was equally possible that the woman might have been in the pension at Christiania. He did not know her.

It is strange that in all such intrigues as his with Angelika the persons concerned are always convinced that they are invisible. He believed that, up to this time, no human being had known anything about it. The merest suspicion that this was not the case made it altogether loathsome.

The pension—Angelika—the letters. He would be hanged if he would go on with it for any earthly inducement. Had Angelika angled for him and landed him like a stupid fat fish? He had been absolutely unsuspicious. The whole affair had been without importance, until they met again at Copenhagen. Perhaps THAT, too, had been a deep-laid plan.

Nothing can more wound a man's vanity than to find that, believing himself a victor, he is in truth a captive.

Rafael paced the deck half the night, and when he reached Christiania went to an hotel, intending to go home the next day to Hellebergene, come what would. This and everything of the kind must end for ever: it simply led straight to the devil. When once he was at home, and could find out where Helene was, the rest would soon be settled.

From the hotel he went up to Angelika Nagel's pension to say that some luggage which was there was to be sent down to the hotel at once—he was leaving that afternoon.

He had dined and gone up to his room to pack, when Angelika stood before him. She was at once so pretty and so sad-looking that he had never seen anything more pathetic.

Had he really kept away from her house? Was he going at once?

She wept so despairingly that he, who was prepared for anything rather than to see her so inconsolable, answered her evasively.

Their relations, he said, had had no more significance than a chance meeting. This they both understood; therefore she must realise that, sooner or later, it must end. And now the time was come.

Indeed, it had more significance, she said. There had never been any one to whom she had been so much attached; this she had proved to him. Now she had come here to tell him that she was enceinte. She was in as great despair about it as any one could be. It was ruin for herself and her children. She had never contemplated anything so frightful, but her mad love had carried her away; so now she was where she deserved to be.

Rafael did not answer, for he could not collect his thoughts. She sat at a table, her face buried in her hands, but his eye fell on her strong arms in the close-fitting sleeves, her little foot thrust from beneath her dress; he saw how her whole frame was shaken by sobs. Nevertheless, what first made him collect his thoughts was not sympathy with her who was here before him; it was the thought of Helene, of the Dean, of his mother: what would THEY say?

As though she were conscious whither his thoughts had flown, she raised her head. "Will you really go away from me?" What despair was in her face! The strong woman was weaker than a child.

He stood erect before her, beside his open trunk. He, too, was absolutely miserable.

"What good will it do for me to stay here?" he asked gently.

Her eyes fixed themselves on him, dilating, becoming clearer every moment. Her mouth grew scornful. She seemed to grow taller every moment.

"You will marry me if you are an honourable man!"

"Marry—you?" he exclaimed, first startled, then disdainful. An evil expression came into her eyes; she thrust her head forward; the whole woman collected herself for the attack like a tiger-cat, but it ended with a violent blow on the table.

"Yes you SHALL, devil take me!" she whispered.

She rushed past him to the window. What was she going to do?

She opened it, screamed out he could not clearly hear what, leant far out, and screamed again; then closed it, and turned towards him, threatening, triumphant. He was as white as a sheet, not because he was frightened or dreaded her threats, but because he recognised in her a mortal enemy. He braced himself for the struggle.

She saw this at once. She was conscious of his strength before he had made a movement. There was that in his eye, in his whole demeanour, which SHE would never be able to overcome: a look of determination which one would not willingly contest. If he had not understood her till now, he had equally revealed himself to her.

All the more wildly did she love him. He rejoiced that he had taken no notice of what she had done, but turned to put the last things into his trunk and fasten it. Then she came close up to him, in more complete contrition, penitence, and wretchedness than he had ever seen in life or art. Her face stiffened with terror, her eyes fixed, her whole frame rigid, only her tears flowed quietly, without a sob. She must and would have him. She seemed to draw him to herself as into a vortex: her love had become the necessity of her life, its utterances the wild cry of despair.

He understood it now. But he put the things into his trunk and fastened it, took a few steps about the room, as if he were alone, with such an expression of face that she herself saw that the thing was impossible.

"Do you not believe," she said quietly, "that I would relieve you of all cares, so that you could go on with your own work? Have you not seen that I can manage your mother?" She paused a moment, then added: "Hellebergene—I know the place. The Dean is a relation of mine. I have been there; that would be something that I could take charge of; do you not think so? And the cement quarries," she added; "I have a turn for business: it should be no trouble to you." She said this in an undertone. She had a slight lisp, which gave her an air of helplessness. "Don't go away, to-day, at any rate. Think it over," she added, weeping bitterly again.

He felt that he ought to comfort her.

She came towards him, and throwing her arms round him, she clung to him in her despair and eagerness. "Don't go, don't go!" She felt that he was yielding. "Never," she whispered, "since I have been a widow have I given myself to any one but you; and so judge for yourself." She laid her head on his shoulder and sobbed bitterly.

"It has come upon me so suddenly," he said; "I cannot—"

"Then take time," she interrupted in a whisper, and took a hasty kiss. "Oh, Rafael!" She twined her arms round him: her touch thrilled through him—

Some one knocked at the door: they started away from each other. It was the man who had come for the luggage. Rafael flushed crimson. "I shall not go till to-morrow," he said.

When the man had left the room Angelika sprang towards Rafael. She thanked and kissed him. Oh, how she beamed with delight and exultation! She was like a girl of twenty, or rather like a young man, for there was something masculine in her manner as she left him.

But the light and fire were no sooner withdrawn than his spirits fell. A little later he lay at full length on the sofa, as though in a grave. He felt as though he could never get up from it again. What was his life now? For there is a dream in every life which is its soul, and when the dream is gone the life appears a corpse.

This, then, was the fulfilment of his forebodings. Hither the ravens had followed the wild beast which dwelt in him. It would on longer play and amuse him, but strike its claws into him in earnest, overthrow him, and lap his fresh-spilt blood.

But it was none the less certain that if he left her she would be ruined, she and her child. Then no one would consider him as an honourable man, least of all himself.

During his last sojourn in France, when he could not settle down to a great work which was constantly dawning before him, he had thought to himself—You have taken life too lightly. Nothing great ever comes to him who does so.

Now, perhaps, when he did his duty here; took upon himself the burden of his fault towards her, himself, and others—and bore it like a man; then perhaps he would be able to utilise all his powers. That was what his mother had done, and she had succeeded.

But with the thought of his mother came the thought of Helene, of his dream. It was flying from him like a bird of passage from the autumn. He lay there and felt as though he could never get up again.

From amid the turmoil of the last summer there came to his recollection two individuals, in whom he reposed entire confidence: a young man and his wife. He went to see them the same evening and laid the facts honestly before them, for now, at all events, he was honest. The conclusive proof of being so is to be able to tell everything about oneself as he did now.

They heard him with dismay, but their advice was remarkable. He ought to wait and see if she were enceinte.

This aroused his spirit of contradiction. There was no doubt about it, for she was perfectly truthful. But she might be mistaken; she ought to make quite sure. This suggestion, too, shocked him; but he agreed that she should come and talk things over with them. They knew her.

She came the next day. They said to her, what they could not very well say to Rafael, that she would ruin him. The wife especially did not spare her. A highly gifted young man like Rafael Kaas, with such excellent prospects in every way, must not, when little more than twenty, burden himself with a middle-aged wife and a number of children. He was far from rich, he had told her so himself; his life would be that of a beast of burden, and that too, before he had learned to bear the yoke. If he had to work, to feed so many people, he might strain himself to the uttermost, he would still remain mediocre. They would both suffer under this, be disappointed and discontented. He must not pay so heavy a price for an indiscretion for which she was ten times more to blame than he. What did she imagine people would say? He who was so popular, so sought after. They would fall upon her like rooks at a rooks' parliament and pick her to pieces. They would, without exception, believe the worst.

The husband asked her if she were quite sure that she was enceinte: she ought to make quite certain.

Angelika Nazel reddened, and answered, half scornful, half laughing, that she ought to know.

"Yes," he retorted, "many people have said that—who were mistaken. If it is understood that you are to be married on account of your condition, and it should afterwards turn out that you were mistaken, what do you suppose that people will say? for of course it will get about."

She reddened again and sprang to her feet. "They can say what they please." After a pause she added: "But God knows I do not wish to make him unhappy."

To conceal her emotion she turned away from them, but the wife would not give up. She suggested that Angelika should write to Rafael without further delay, to set him free and let him return home to his mother; there they would be able to arrange matters. Angelika was so capable that she could earn a living anywhere. Rafael too ought to help her.

"I shall write to his mother," Angelika said. "She shall know all about it, so that she may understand for what he is responsible."

This they thought reasonable, and Angelika sat down and wrote. She frequently showed agitation, but she went on quickly, steadily, sheet after sheet. Just then came a ring—a messenger with a letter. The maid brought it in. Her mistress was about to take it, but it was not for her; it was for Angelika—they both recognised Rafael's careless handwriting.

Angelika opened it—grew crimson; for he wrote that the result of his most serious considerations was, that neither she nor her children should be injured by him. He was an honourable man who would bear his own responsibilities, not let others be burdened by them.

Angelika handed the letter to her friend, then tore up the one which she had been writing, and left the house.

Her friend stood thinking to herself—The good that is in us must go bail for the evil, so we must rest and be satisfied.

The discovery which she had made had often been made before, but it was none the less true.

CHAPTER 5

The next day they were married. That night, long after his wife had fallen into her usual healthy sleep, Rafael thought sorrowfully of his lost Paradise. HE could not sleep. As he lay there he seemed to look out over a meadow, which had no springtime, and therefore no flowers. He retraced the events of the past day. His would be a marred life which had never known the sweet joys of courtship.

Angelika did not share his beliefs. She was a stern realist, a sneering sceptic, in the most literal sense a cynic.

Her even breathing, her regular features, seemed to answer him. "Hey-dey, my boy, we shall be merry for a thousand years! Better sleep now, you will need sleep if you mean to try which of us is the stronger."

The next day their marriage was the marvel of the town and neighbourhood.

"Just like his mother!" people exclaimed; "what promise there was in her! She might have chosen so as to have been now in one of the best positions in the country—when, lo and behold! she went and made the most idiotic marriage. The most idiotic? No, the son's is more idiotic still." And so on and so forth.

Most people seem naturally impelled to exalt the hero of the hour higher than they themselves intend, and when a reaction comes, to decry him in an equal degree. Few people see with their own eyes, and on special occasions even magnifying or diminishing glasses are called into play with most amusing results.

"Rafael Kaas a handsome fellow?—well, yes, but too big, too fair, no repose, altogether too restless. Rich? He? He has not a stiver! The savings eaten up long ago, nothing coming in, they have been encroaching on their capital for some time; and the beds of cement stone—who the deuce would join with him in any large undertaking? They talk about his gifts, his genius even; but IS he very highly gifted? Is it anything more than what he has acquired? The saving of motive power at the factory? Was that anything more than a mere repetition of what he had done before?—and that, of course, only what he had seen elsewhere."

Just the same with the hints which he had given. "Merely close personal observation; for it must be admitted that he had more of that than most people; but as for ingenuity! Well, he could make out a good case for himself, but that was about the extent of his ingenuity."

"His earlier articles, as well as those which had recently appeared on the use of electricity in baking and tanning—could you call those discoveries? Let us see what he will invent now that he has come home, and cannot get ideas from reading and from seeing people."

Rafael noticed this change—first among the ladies, who all seemed to have been suddenly blown away, with a few exceptions, who did not respect a marriage like his, and who would not give in.

His relations, also, held somewhat aloof. "It was not thus that he showed himself a true Ravn. He was so in temperament and disposition, perhaps, but it was just his defect that he was only a half-breed."

The change of front was complete: he noticed it on all hands. But he was man enough, and had sufficient obstinacy as well, to let himself be urged on by this to hard work, and in his wife there was still more of the same feeling.

He had a sense of elevation in having done his duty, and as long as this tension lasted it kept him up to the mark. On the day of his marriage (from early in the morning until the time when the ceremony took place) he employed himself in writing to his mother; a wonderful, a solemn letter in the sight of the All-Knowing,—the cry of a tortured soul in utmost peril.

It depended on his mother whether she would receive them and let their life become all that was now possible. Angelika—their business, manager, housekeeper, chief. He—devoted to his experiments. She—the tender mother, the guide of both.

It seemed to him that their future depended on this letter and the answer to it, and he wrote in that spirit. Never had he so fully depicted himself, so fully searched his own heart.

It was the outcome of what he had lived through during these last few days, the mellowing influence of his struggles during the night watches. Nothing could have been more candid.

He was pained that he did not receive an answer at once, although he realised what a blow it would be to her. He understood that, to begin with, it would destroy all her dreams, as it had already destroyed. But he relied on her optimistic nature, which he had never known surpassed, and on the depth of her purpose in all that she undertook. He knew that she drew strength and resolution from all that was deepest in their common life.

Therefore he gave her time, notwithstanding Angelika's restlessness, which could hardly be controlled. She even began to sneer; but there was something holy in his anticipation: her words fell unheeded.

When on the third day he had received no letter, he telegraphed, merely these words: "Mother, send me an answer." The wires had never carried anything more fraught with unspoken grief.

He could not return home. He remained alone outside the town until the evening, by which time the answer might well have arrived. It was there.

"My beloved son, YOU are always welcome; most of all when you are unhappy!" The word YOU was underlined. He grew deadly pale, and went slowly into his own room. There Angelika let him remain for a while in peace, then came in and lit the lamp. He could see that she was much agitated, and that every now and then she cast hasty glances at him.

"Do you know what, Rafael? you ought simply to go straight to your mother. It is too bad, both on account of our future and hers. We shall be ruined by gossip and trash."

He was too unhappy to be contemptuous. She had no respect for anybody or anything, he thought; why, then, should he be angry because she felt none, either for his mother or for his position in regard to her? But how vulgar Angelika seemed to him, as she bent over a troublesome lamp and let her impatience break out! Her mouth but too easily acquired a coarse expression. Her small head would rear itself above her broad shoulders with a snake-like expression, and her thick wrist—

"Well," she said, "when all is said and done, that disgusting Hellebergene is not worth making a fuss over."

Now she is annoyed with herself, he thought, and must have her say. She will not rest until she has picked a quarrel; but she shall not have that satisfaction.

"After all that has been said and all that has happened there—"

But this, too, missed fire. "How could I have supposed that she could manage my mother?" He got up and paced the room. "Is that what mother felt? Yet they were such good friends. I suspected nothing then. How is it that mother's instinct is always more delicate? have I blunted mine?"

When, a little later, Angelika came in again, he looked so unhappy that she was struck by it, and she then showed herself so kind and fertile in resource on his behalf, and there was such sunshine in her cheerfulness and flow of spirits during the evening, that he actually brightened up under it, and thought—If mother could have brought herself to try the experiment, perhaps after all it might have answered. There is so much that is good and capable in this curious creature.

He went to the children. From the first day he and they had taken to each other. They had been unhappy in the great pension, with a mother who seldom came near them or took any notice of them, except as clothes to be patched, mouths to feed, or faults to be punished.

Rafael had in his nature the unconventionality which delights in children's confidence, and he felt a desire to love and to be loved. Children are quick to feel this.

They only wasted Angelika's time. They were in her way now more than ever; for it may be said at once that, Rafael had become EVERYTHING to her. This was the fascination in her, and whatever happened, it never lost its power. Her tenderness, her devotion, were boundless. By the aid of her personal charm, her resourceful ingenuity, she obtained every advantage for him within her range, and even beyond it. It was felt in her devotion by night and day, when anything was to be done, in an untiring zeal such as only so strong and healthy a woman could have had in her power to render. But in words it did not show itself, hardly even in looks: except, perhaps, while she fought to win him, but never since then.

Had she been able to adhere to one line of conduct, if only for a few weeks at a time, and let herself be guided by her never-failing love, he would, in this stimulating atmosphere, have made of his married life what his mother, in spite of all, had made of hers.

Why did not this happen? Because the jealousy which she had aroused in him and which had drawn him to her again was now reversed.

They were hardly married before it was she who was jealous! Was it strange? A middle-aged woman, even though she be endowed with the strongest personality and the widest sympathy, when she wins a young husband who is the fashion—wins him as Angelika won hers—begins to live in perpetual disquietude lest any one should take him from her. Had she not taken him herself?

If we were to say that she was jealous of every human being who came there, man or woman, old or young, beside those whom he met elsewhere, it would be an exaggeration, but this exaggeration throws a strong light upon the state of things, which actually existed.

If he became at all interested in conversation with any one, she always interrupted. Her face grew hard, her right foot began to move; and if this did not suffice, she struck in with sulky or provoking remarks, no matter who was there.

If something were said in praise of any one, and it seemed to excite his interest, she would pooh-pooh it, literally with a "pooh!" a shrug of the shoulders, a toss of the head, or an impatient tap of the foot.

At first he imagined that she really knew something disadvantageous about all those whom she thus disparaged, and he was filled with admiration at her acquaintance with half Norway. He believed in her veracity as he believed in few things. He believed, too, that it was unbounded like so many of her qualities. She said the most cynical things in the plainest manner without apparent design.

But little by little it dawned upon him that she said precisely what it pleased her to say, according to the humour that she was in.

One day, as they were going to table—he had come in late and was hungry— he was delighted to see that there were oysters.

"Oysters! at this time of the year," he cried. "They must be very expensive."

"Pooh! that was the old woman, you know. She persuaded me to take them for you. I got them for next to nothing."

"That was odd; you have been out, then, too?"

"Yes, and I saw YOU; you were walking with Emma Ravn."

He understood at once, by the tone of her voice, that this was not permitted, but all the same he said, "Yes; how sweet she is! so fresh and candid."

"She! Why, she had a child before she was married."

"Emma? Emma Ravn?"

"Yes! But I do not know who by."

"Do you know, Angelika, I do not believe that," he said solemnly.

"You can do as you please about that, but she was at the pension at the time, so you can judge for yourself if I am right."

He could not believe that any human being could so belie themselves. Emma's eyes, clear as water in a fountain where one can count the pebbles at the bottom, rose to his mind, in all their innocence. He could not believe that such eyes could lie. He grew livid, he could not eat, he left the table. The world was nothing but a delusion, the purest was impure.

For a long time after this, whenever he met Emma or her white-haired mother, he turned aside, so as not to come face to face with them.

He had clung to his relations: their weak points were apparent to every one, but their ability and honesty no less so. This one story destroyed his confidence, impaired his self-reliance, shattered his belief, and thus made him the poorer. How could he be fit for anything, when he so constantly allowed himself to be befooled?

There was not one word of truth in the whole story.

His simple confidence was held in her grasp, like a child in the talons of an eagle; but this did not last much longer.

Fortunately, she was without calculation or perseverance. She did not remember one day what she had said the day before; for each day she coolly asserted whatever was demanded by the necessity of the moment. He, on the contrary, had an excellent memory; and his mathematical mind ranged the evidence powerfully against her. Her gifts were more aptness and quickness than anything else, they were without training, without cohesion, and permeated with passion at all points. Therefore he could, at any moment, crush her defence; but whenever this happened, it was so evident that she had been actuated by jealousy that it flattered his vanity; which was the reason why he did not regard it seriously enough — did not pursue his advantage. Perhaps if he had done so, he would have discovered more, for this jealousy was merely the form which her uneasiness took. This uneasiness arose from several causes.

The fact was that she had a past and she had debts which she had denied, and now she lived in perpetual dread lest any one should enlighten him. If any one got on the scent, she felt sure that this would be used against her. It merely depended on what he learned — in other words, with whom he associated.

She could disregard anonymous letters because he did so, but there were plenty of disagreeable people who might make innuendoes.

She saw that Rafael too, to some extent, avoided his countless friends of old days. She did not understand the reason, but it was this: that he, as well, felt that they knew more of her than it was expedient for HIM to know. She saw that he made ingenious excuses for not being seen out with her. This, too, she misconstrued. She did not at all understand that he, in his way, was quite as frightened as she was of what people might say. She believed that he sought the society of others rather than hers. If nothing more came of such intercourse, stories might be told. This was the reason for her slanders about almost every one he spoke to. If they had vilified her, they must be vilified in return.

She had debts, and this could not be concealed unless she increased them; this she did with a boldness worthy of a better cause. The house was kept on an extravagant scale, with an excellent table and great hospitality. Otherwise he would not be comfortable at home, she said and believed.

She herself vied with the most fashionably dressed ladies in the town. Her daily struggle to maintain her hold on him demanded this. It followed, of course, that she got everything for "nothing" or "the greatest bargain in the world." There was always some one "who almost gave it" to her. He did not know himself how much money he spent, perhaps, because she hunted and drove him from one thing to another.

Originally he had thought of going abroad; but with a wife who knew no foreign languages, with a large family—

Here at home, as he soon discovered, every one had lost confidence in him. He dared not take up anything important, or else he wished to wait a little before he came to any definite determination. In the meantime, he did whatever came to hand, and that was often work of a subordinate description. Both from weariness, and from the necessity to earn a living, he ended by doing only mediocre work, and let things drift.

He always gave out that this was only "provisional." His scientific gifts, his inventive genius, with so many pounds on his back, did not rise high, but they should yet! He had youth's lavish estimate of time and strength, and therefore did not see, for a long time, that the large family, the large house were weighing him farther and farther down. If only he could have a little peace, he thought, he would carry out his present ideas and new ones also. He felt such power within him.

But peace was just what he never had. Now we come to the worst, or more properly, to the sum of what has gone before. The ceaseless uneasiness in which Angelika lived broke out into perpetual quarrelling. For one thing, she had no self-command. A caprice, a mistake, an anxiety over-ruled everything. She seized the smallest opportunities. Again—and this was a most important factor—there was her overpowering anxiety to keep possession of him; this drew her away from what she should have paid most heed to, in order to let him have peace. She continued her lavish housekeeping, she let the children drift, she concentrated all her powers on him. Her jealousy, her fears, her debts, sapped his fertile mind, destroyed his good humour, laid desolate his love of the beautiful and his creative power.

He had in particular one great project, which he had often, but ineffectually, attempted to mature. The effort to do so had begun seriously one day on the heights above Hellebergene, and had continued the whole summer. Curiously enough, one morning, as he sat at some most wearisome work, Hellebergene and Helene, in the spring sunshine, rose before him, and with them his project, lofty and smiling, came to him again. Then he begged for a little peace in the house.

"Let me be quiet, if only for a month," he said. "Here is some money. I have got an idea; I must and will have quiet. In a month's time I shall have got on so far that perhaps I shall be able to judge if it is worth continuing. It may be that this one idea may entirely support us."

This was something which she could understand, and now he was able to be quiet.

He had an office in the town, but sometimes took his papers home with him in the evenings, for it often happened that something would occur to him at one moment or another. She bestowed every care on him; she even sat on the stairs while he was asleep at midday, to prevent him from being disturbed.

This went on for a fortnight. Then it so chanced that, when he had gone out for a walk, she rummaged among his papers, and there, among drawings, calculations, and letters, she actually, for once in a way, found something. It was in his handwriting and as follows:

"More of the mother than the lover in her; more of the solicitude of love than of its enjoyment. Rich in her affection, she would not squander it in one day with you, but, mother-like, would distribute it throughout your life. Instead of the whirl of the rapids, a placid stream. Her love was devotion, never absorption. YOU were one and SHE was one. Together we should have been more powerful than two lovers are wont to be."

There was more of this, but Angelika could not read further, she became so furious. Were these his own thoughts, or had he merely copied them? There were no corrections, so most likely it was a copy. In any case it showed where his thoughts were.

Rafael came quietly home, went straight to his room and lighted a candle, even before he took off his overcoat. As he stood he wrote down a few formulae, then seized a book, sat down astride of a chair, and made a rapid calculation. Just then Angelika came in, leaned forward towards him, and said in a low voice:

"You are a nice fellow! Now I know what you have in hand. Look there: your secret thoughts are with that beast."

"Beast!" he repeated. His anger at being disturbed, at her having found this particular paper, and now the abuse from her coarse lips of the most delicate creature he had ever known, and, above all, the absolute unexpectedness of the attack, made him lose his head.

"How dare you? What do you mean?"

"Don't be a fool. Do you suppose that I don't guess that that is meant for the girl who looked after your estate in order to catch you?"

She saw that this hit the mark, so she went still further.

"She, the model of virtue! why, when she was a mere girl, she disgraced herself with an old man."

As she spoke she was seized by the throat and flung backwards on to the sofa, without the grasp being relaxed. She was breathless, she saw his face over her; deadly rage was in it. A strength, a wildness of which she had no conception, gazed upon her in sensual delight at being able to strangle her.

After a wild struggle her arms sank down powerless, her will with them; only her eyes remained wide open, in terror and wonderment.

Dare he? "Yes, he dare!" Her eyes grew dim, her limbs began to tremble.

"You have taken MY apple, I tell you," was heard in a childish voice from the next room, a soft lisping voice.

It came from the most peaceful innocence in the world! It saved her!

He rushed out again; but even when the rage had left him which had seized upon him and dominated him as a rider does a horse, he was still not horrified at himself. His satisfaction at having at length made his power felt was too great for that.

But by degrees there came a revulsion. Suppose he had killed her, and had to go into penal servitude for the rest of his life for it! Had such a possibility come into his life? Might it happen in the future? No! no! no! How strange that Angelika should have wounded him! How frightful her state of mind must be when she could think so odiously of absolutely innocent people; and how angry she must have been to behave in such a way towards him, whom she loved above all others, indeed, as the only one for whom she had to live!

A long, long sum followed: his faults, her faults, and the faults of others. He cooled down and began to feel more like himself.

In an hour or two he was fit to go home, to find her on her bed, dissolved in tears, prepared at once to throw her arms round his neck.

He asked pardon a hundred times, with words, kisses, and caresses.

But with this scene his invention had fled. The spell was broken. It never did more than flutter before him, tempting him to pursue it once more; but he turned away from the whole subject and began to work for money again. Something offered itself just at that moment which Angelika had hunted up.

Back to the unending toil again. Now at last it became an irritation to him: he chafed as the war horse chafes at being made a beast of burden.

This made the scenes at home still worse. Since that episode their quarrels knew no bounds. Words were no longer necessary to bring them about: a gesture, a look, a remark of his unanswered, was enough to arouse the most violent scenes. Hitherto they had been restrained by the presence of others, but now it was the same whether they were alone or not. Very soon, as far as brutality of expression or the triviality of the question was concerned, he was as bad or worse than she.

His idle fancy and creative genius found no other vent, but overthrew and trampled underfoot many of life's most beautiful gifts. Thus he squandered much of the happiness which such talents can duly give. Sometimes his daily regrets and sufferings, sometimes his passionate nature, were in the ascendant, but the cause of his despair was always the same—that this could have happened to him.

Should he leave her? He would not thus escape. The state of the case had touched his conscience at first, later he had become fond of the children, and his mother's example said to him, "Hold out, hold out!"

The unanimous prediction that this marriage would be dissolved as quickly as it had been made he would prove to be untrue. Besides, he knew Angelika too well now not to know that he would never obtain a separation from her until, with the law at her back, she had flayed him alive. He could not get free.

From the first it had been a question of honour and duty; honour and duty on account of the child which was to come—and which did not come. Here he had a serious grievance against her; but yet, in the midst of the tragedy, he could not but be amused at the skill with which she turned his own gallantries against him. At last he dared not mention the subject, for he only heard in return about his gay bachelor life.

The longer this state of things lasted and the more it became known, the more incomprehensible it became to most people that they did not separate—to himself, too, at times, during sleepless nights. But it is sometimes the case that he, who makes a thousand small revolts, cannot brace himself to one great one. The endless strife itself strengthens the bonds, in that it saps the strength.

He deteriorated. This married life, wearing in every way, together with the hard work, resulted in his not being equal to more than just the necessities of the day. His initiative and will became proportionately deadened.

A strange stagnation developed itself: he had hallucinations, visions; he saw himself in them—his father! his mother! all the pictures were of a menacing description.

At night he dreamed the most frightful things: his unbridled fancy, his unoccupied creative power, took revenge, and all this weakened him. He looked with admiration at his wife's robust health: she had the physique of a wild beast. But at times their quarrels, their reconciliations, brought revelations with them: he could perceive her sorrows as well. She did not complain, she did not say a word, she could not do so; but at times she wept and gave way as only the most despairing can. Her nature was powerful, and the struggle of her love beyond belief. The beauty of the fulness of life was there, even when she was most repulsive. The wild creature, wrestling with her destiny, often gave forth tragic gleams of light.

One day his relation, the Government Secretary, met him. They usually avoided each other, but to-day he stopped.

"Ah, Rafael," said the dapper little man nervously, "I was coming to see you."

"My dear fellow, what is it?"

"Ah, I see that you guess; it is a letter from your mother."

"From my mother?"

During all the time since her telegram they had not exchanged a word.

"A very long letter, but she makes a condition."

"Hum, hum! a condition?"

"Yes, but do not be angry; it is not a hard one: it is only that you are to go away from the town, wherever you like, so long as you can be quiet, and then you are to read it."

"You know the contents?"

"I know the contents, I will go bail for it."

What he meant, or why he was so perturbed by it, Rafael did not understand, but it infected him; if he had had the money, and if on that day he had been disengaged, he would have gone at once. But he had not the money, not more than he wanted for the fete that evening. He had the tickets for it in his pocket at that moment. He had promised Angelika that he would go there with her, and he would keep his promise, for it had been given after a great reconciliation scene. A white silk dress had been the olive branch of these last peaceful days. She therefore looked very handsome that evening as she walked into the great hall of the Lodge, with Rafael beside her tall and stately. She was in excellent spirits. Her quiet eyes had a haughty expression as she turned her steps with confident superiority towards those whom she wished to please, or those whom she hoped to annoy.

HE did not feel confident. He did not like showing himself in public with her, and lately it had precisely been in public places that she had chosen to make scenes; besides which, he felt nervous as to what his mother could wish to say to him.

A short time before he came to the fete, he had tried, in two quarters, to borrow money, and each time had received only excuses. This had greatly mortified him. His disturbed state of mind, as is so often the case with nervous people, made him excited and boisterous, nay, even made him more than usually jovial. And as though a little of the old happiness were actually to come to him that evening, he met his friend and relative Hans Ravn, him and his young Bavarian wife, who had just come to the town. All three were delighted to meet.

"Do you remember," said Hans Ravn, "how often you have lent me money, Rafael?" and he drew him on one side. "Now I am at the top of the tree, now I am married to an heiress, and the most charming girl too; ah, you must know her better."

"She is pretty as well," said Rafael.

"And pretty as well—and good tempered; in fact, you see before you the happiest man in Norway."

Rafael's eyes filled. Ravn put his hands on to his friend's shoulders.

"Are you not happy, Rafael?"

"Not quite so happy as you, Hans—"

He left him to speak to some one else, then returned again.

"You say, Hans, that I have often lent you money."

"Are you pressed? Do you want some, Rafael? My dear fellow, how much?"

"Can you spare me two thousand kroner?"

"Here they are."

"No, no; not in here, come outside."

"Yes, let us go and have some champagne to celebrate our meeting. No, not our wives," he added, as Rafael looked towards where they stood talking.

"Not our wives," laughed Rafael. He understood the intention, and now he wished to enjoy his freedom thoroughly. They came in again merrier and more boisterous than before.

Rafael asked Hans Ravn's young wife to dance. Her personal attractions, natural gaiety, and especially her admiration of her husband's relations, took him by storm. They danced twice, and laughed and talked together afterwards.

Later in the evening the two friends rejoined their wives, so that they might all sit together at supper. Even from a distance Rafael could see by Angelika's face that a storm was brewing. He grew angry at once. He had never been blamed more groundlessly. He was never to have any unalloyed pleasure, then! But he confined himself to whispering, "Try to behave like other people." But that was exactly what she did not mean to do. He had left her alone, every one had seen it. She would have her revenge. She could not endure Hans Ravn's merriment, still less that of his wife, so she contradicted rudely once, twice, three times, while Hans Ravn's face grew more and more puzzled. The storm might have blown over, for Rafael parried each thrust, even turning them into jokes, so that the party grew merrier, and no feelings were hurt; but on this she tried fresh tactics. As has been already said, she could make a number of annoying gestures, signs and movements which only he understood. In this way she showed him her contempt for everything which every one, and especially he himself, said. He could not help looking towards her, and saw this every time he did so, until under the cover of the laughter of the others, with as much fervour and affection as can be put into such a word, "You jade!" he said.

"Jade; was ist das?" asked the bright-eyed foreigner.

This made the whole affair supremely ridiculous. Angelika herself laughed, and all hoped that the cloud had been finally dispersed. No!—as though Satan himself had been at table with them, she would not give in.

The conversation again grew lively, and when it was at its height, she pooh-poohed all their jokes so unmistakably that they were completely puzzled. Rafael gave her a furious look, and then she jeered at him, "You boy!" she said. After this Rafael answered her angrily, and let nothing pass without retaliation, rough, savage retaliation; he was worse than she was.

"But God bless me!" said good-natured Hans Ravn at length, "how you are altered, Rafael!" His genial kindly eyes gazed at him with a look which Rafael never forget.

"Ja, ich kan es nicht mehr aushalten" said the young Fru Ravn, with tears in her eyes. She rose, her husband hurried to her, and they left together. Rafael sat down again, with Angelika. Those near them looked towards them and whispered together. Angry and ashamed, he looked across at Angelika, who laughed. Everything seemed to turn red before his eyes—he rose; he had a wild desire to kill her there, before every one. Yes! the temptation overpowered him to such an extent that he thought that people must notice it.

"Are you not well, Kaas?" he heard some one beside him say.

He could not remember afterwards what he answered, or how he got away; but still, in the street, he dwelt with ecstasy on the thought of killing her, of again seeing her face turn black, her arms fall powerless, her eyes open wide with terror; for that was what would happen some day. He should end his life in a felon's cell. That was as certainly a part of his destiny as had been the possession of talents which he had allowed to become useless.

A quarter of an hour later he was at the observatory: he scanned the heavens, but no stars were visible. He felt that he was perspiring, that his clothes clung to him, yet he was ice-cold. That is the future that awaits you, he thought; it runs ice-cold through your limbs.

Then it was that a new and, until then, unused power, which underlay all else, broke forth and took the command.

"You shall never return home to her, that is all past now, boy; I will not permit it any longer."

What was it? What voice was that? It really sounded as though outside himself. Was it his father's? It was a man's voice. It made him clear and calm. He turned round, he went straight to the nearest hotel, without further thought, without anxiety. Something new was about to begin.

He slept for three hours undisturbed by dreams; it was the first night for a long time that he had done so.

The following morning he sat in the little pavilion at the station at Eidsvold with his mother's packet of letters laid open before him. It consisted of a quantity of papers which he had read through.

The expanse of Lake Mjosen lay cold and grey beneath the autumn mist, which still shrouded the hillsides. The sound of hammers from the workshops to the right mingled with the rumble of wheels on the bridge; the whistle of an engine, the rattle of crockery from the restaurant; sights and sounds seethed round him like water boiling round an egg.

As soon as his mother had felt sure that Angelika was not really enceinte she had busied herself in collecting all the information about her which it was possible to obtain.

By the untiring efforts of her ubiquitous relations she had succeeded to such an extent and in such detail as no examining magistrate could have accomplished. And there now lay before him letters, explanations, evidence, which the deponent was ready to swear to, besides letters from Angelika herself: imprudent letters which this impulsive creature could perpetrate in the midst of her schemes; or deeply calculated letters, which directly contradicted others which had been written at a different period, based on different calculations. These documents were only the accompaniment of a clear summing-up by his mother. It was therefore she who had guided the investigations of the others and made a digest of their discoveries. With mathematical precision was here laid down both what was certain and what, though not certain, was probable. No comment was added, not a word addressed to himself.

That portion of the disclosures which related to Angelika's past does not concern us. That which had reference to her relations with Rafael began by proving that the anonymous letters, which had been the means of preventing his engagement with Helene, had been written by Angelika. This revelation and that which preceded it, give an idea of the overwhelming humiliation under which Rafael now suffered. What was he that he could be duped and mastered like a captured animal; that what was best and what was worst in him could lead him so far astray? Like a weak fool he was swept along; he had neither seen nor heard nor thought before he was dragged away from everything that was his or that was dear to him.

As he sat there, the perspiration poured from him as it had done the night before, and again he felt a deadly chill. He therefore went up to his room with the papers, which he locked up in his trunk, and then set off at a run along the road. The passers-by turned to stare after the tall fellow.

As he ran he repeated to himself, "Who are you, my lad? who are you?" Then he asked the hills the same question, and then the trees as well. He even asked the fog, which was now rolling off, "Who am I? can you answer me that?"

The close-cropped half-withered turf mocked him — the cleared potato patches, the bare fields, the fallen leaves.

"That which you are you will never be; that which you can you will never do; that which you ought to become you will never attain to! As you, so your mother before you. She turned aside — and your father too — into absolute folly; perhaps their fathers before them! This is a branch of a great family who never attained to what they were intended for."

"Something different has misled each one of us, but we have all been misled. Why is that so? We have greater aims than many others, but the others drove along the beaten highway right through the gates of Fortune's house. We stray away from the highway and into the wood. See! am I not there myself now? Away from the highway and into the wood, as though I were led by an inward law. Into the wood." He looked round among the mountain-ashes, the birches, and other leafy trees in autumn tints. They stood all round, dripping, as though they wept for his sorrow. "Yes, yes; they will see me hang here, like Absalom by his long hair." He had not recalled this old picture a moment before he stopped, as though seized by a strong hand.

He must not fly from this, but try to fathom it. The more he thought of it, the clearer it became: ABSALOM'S HISTORY WAS HIS OWN. He began with rebellion. Naturally rebellion is the first step in a course which leads one from the highway — leads to passion and its consequences. That was clear enough.

Thus passion overpowered strength of purpose; thus chance circumstances sapped the foundations—But David rebelled as well. Why, then, was not David hung up by his hair? It was quite as long as Absalom's. Yes, David was within an ace of it, right up to his old age. But the innate strength in David was too great, his energy was always too powerful: it conquered the powers of rebellion. They could not drag him far away into passionate wanderings; they remained only holiday flights in his life and added poetry to it. They did not move his strength of purpose. Ah, ha! It was so strong in David that he absorbed them and fed on them; and yet he was within an ace—very often. See! That is what I, miserable contemptible wretch, cannot do. So I must hang! Very soon the man with the spear will be after me.

Rafael now set off running; probably he wished to escape the man with the spear. He now entered the thickest part of the wood, a narrow valley between two high hills which overshadowed it. Oh, how thirsty he was, so fearfully thirsty! He stood still and wondered whether he could get anything to drink. Yes, he could hear the murmur of a brook. He ran farther down towards it. Close by was an opening in the wood, and as he went towards the stream he was arrested by something there: the sun had burst forth and lighted up the tree-tops, throwing deep shadows below. Did he see anything? Yes; it seemed to him that he saw himself, not absolutely in the opening, but to one side, in the shadow, under a tree; he hung there by his hair. He hung there and swung, a man, but in the velvet jacket of his childhood and the tight-fitting trousers: he swung suspended by his tangled red hair. And farther away he distinctly saw another figure: it was his mother, stiff and stately, who was turning round as if to the sound of music. And, God preserve him! still farther away, broad and heavy, hung his father, by the few thin hairs on his neck, with wretched distorted face as on his death-bed. In other respects those two were not great sinners. They were old; but his sins were great, for he was young, and therefore nothing had ever prospered with him, not even in his childhood. There had always been something which had caused him to be misunderstood or which had frightened him or made him constantly constrained and uncertain of himself. Never had he been able to keep to the main point, and thus to be in quiet natural peace. With only one exception—his meeting with Helene.

It seemed to him that he was sitting in the boat with her out in the bay. The sky was bright, there was melody in the woods. Now he was up on the hill with her, among the saplings, and she was explaining to him that it depended on her care whether they throve or not.

He went to the brook to drink; he lay down over the water. He was thus able to see his own face. How could that happen? Why, there was sunshine overhead. He was able to see his own face. Great heavens! how like his father he had become. In the last year he had grown very like his father—people had said so. He well remembered his mother's manner when she noticed it. But, good God! were those grey hairs? Yes, in quantities, so that his hair was no longer red but grey. No one had told him of it. Had he advanced so far, been so little prepared for it, that Hans Ravn's remark, "How you are altered, Rafael!" had frightened him?

He had certainly given up observing himself, in this coarse life of quarrels. In it, certainly, neither words nor deeds were weighed, and hence this hunted feeling. It was only natural that he had ceased to observe. If the brook had been a little deeper, he would have let himself be engulfed in it. He got up, and went on again, quicker and quicker: sometimes he saw one person, sometimes another, hanging in the woods.

He dare not turn round. Was it so very wonderful that others besides himself and his family had turned from the beaten track, and peopled the byways and the boughs in the wood? He had been unjust towards himself and his parents; they were not alone, they were in only too large a company. What will unjust people say, but that the very thing which requires strength does not receive it, but half of it comes to nothing, more than half of the powers are wasted. Here, in these strips of woodland which run up the hills side by side, like organ-pipes, Henrik Vergeland had also roamed: within an ace, with him too, within an ace! Wonderful how the ravens gather together here, where so many people are hanging. Ha! ha! He must write this to his mother! It was something to write about to her, who had left him, who deserted him when he was the most unhappy, because all that she cared for was to keep her sacred person inviolate, to maintain her obstinate opinion, to gratify her pique—Oh! what long hair!—How fast his mother was held! She had not cut her hair enough then. But now she should have her deserts. Everything from as far back as he could remember should be recalled, for once in a way he would show her herself; now he had both the power and the right. His powers of discovery had been long hidden under the suffocating sawdust of the daily and nightly sawing; but now it was awake, and his mother should feel it.

People noticed the tall man break out of the wood, jump over hedges and ditches, and make his way straight up the hill. At the very top he would write to his mother!—

He did not return to the hotel till dark. He was wet, dirty, and frightfully exhausted. He was as hungry as a wolf, he said, but he hardly ate anything; on the other hand, he was consumed with thirst. On leaving the table he said that he wished to stay there a few days to sleep. They thought that he was joking, but he slept uninterruptedly until the afternoon of the next day. He was then awakened, ate a little and drank a great deal, for he had perspired profusely; after which he fell asleep again. He passed the next twenty-four hours in much the same way.

When he awoke the following morning he found himself alone.

Had not a doctor been there, and had he not said that it was a good thing for him to sleep? It seemed to him that he had heard a buzz of voices; but he was sure that he was well now, only furiously hungry and thirsty, and when he raised himself he felt giddy. But that passed off by degrees, when he had eaten some of the food which had been left there. He drank out of the water-jug—the carafe was empty—and walked once or twice up and down before the open window. It was decidedly cold, so he shut it. Just then he remembered that he had written a frightful letter to his mother!

How long ago was it? Had he not slept a long time? Had he not turned grey? He went to the looking-glass, but forgot the grey hair at the sight of himself. He was thin, lank, and dirty.—The letter! the letter! It will kill my mother! There had already been misfortunes enough, more must not follow.

He dressed himself quickly, as if by hurrying he could overtake the letter. He looked at the clock—it had stopped. Suppose the train were in! He must go by it, and from the train straight to the steamer, and home, home to Hellebergene! But he must send a telegram to his mother at once. He wrote it—"Never mind the letter, mother. I am coming this evening and will never leave you again."

So now he had only to put on a clean collar, now his watch—it certainly was morning—now to pack, go down and pay the bill, have something to eat, take his ticket, send the telegram; but first—no, it must all be done together, for the train WAS there; it had only a few minutes more to wait; he could only just catch it. The telegram was given to some one else to send off.

But he had hardly got into the carriage, where he was alone, than the thought of the letter tortured him, till he could not sit still. This dreadful analysis of his mother, strophe after strophe, it rose before him, it again drove him into the state of mind in which he had been among the hills and woods of Eidsvold. Beyond the tunnel the character of the scenery was the same.—Good God! that dreadful letter was never absent from his thoughts, otherwise he would not suffer so terribly. What right had he to reproach his mother, or any one, because a mere chance should have become of importance in their lives?

Would the telegram arrive in time to save her from despair, and yet not frighten her from home because he was coming? To think that he could write in such a way to her, who had but lived to collect the information which would free him! His ingratitude must appear too monstrous to her. The extreme reserve which she was unable to break through might well lead to catastrophes. What might not she have determined on when she received this violent attack by way of thanks? Perhaps she would think that life was no longer worth living, she who thought it so easy to die. He shuddered.

But she will do nothing hastily, she will weigh everything first. Her roots go deep. When she appears to have acted on impulse, it is because she has had previous knowledge. But she has no previous knowledge here; surely here she will deliberate.

He pictured her as, wrapped in her shawl, she wandered about in dire distress—or with intent gaze reviewing her life and his own, until both appeared to her to have been hopelessly wasted—or pondering where she could best hide herself so that she should suffer no more.

How he loved her! All that had happened had drawn a veil over his eyes, which was now removed.

Now he was on board the steamer which was bearing him home. The weather had become mild and summerlike; it had been raining, but towards evening it began to clear. He would get to Hellebergene in fine weather, and by moonlight. It grew colder; he spoke to no one, nor had he eyes for anything about him.

The image of his mother, wrapped in her long shawl—that was all the company he had. Only his mother! No one but his mother! Suppose the telegram had but frightened her the more—that to see HIM now appeared the worst that could happen. To read such a crushing doom for her whole life, and that from him! She was not so constituted that it could be cancelled by his asking forgiveness and returning to her. On the contrary, it would precipitate the worst, it must do so.

The violent perspiration began again; he had to put on more wraps. His terror took possession of him: he was forced to contemplate the most awful possibilities—to picture to himself what death his mother would choose!

He sprang to his feet and paced up and down. He longed to throw himself into somebody's arms, to cry aloud. But he knew well that he must not let such words escape him.—He HAD to picture her as she handled the guns, until she relinquished the idea of using any of them. Then he imagined her recalling the deepest hiding-places in the woods—where were they all?

HE recalled them, one after another. No, not in any of THOSE, for she wished to hide herself where she would never be found! There was the cement-bed; it went sheer down there, and the water was deep!—He clung to the rigging to prevent himself from falling. He prayed to be released from these terrors. But he saw her floating there, rocked by the rippling water. Was it the face which was uppermost, or was it the body, which for a while floated higher than the face?

His thoughts were partially diverted from this by people coming up to ask him if he were ill. He got something warm and strong to drink, and now the steamer approached the part of the coast with which he was familiar. They passed the opening into Hellebergene, for one has to go first to the town, and thence in a boat. It now became the question, whether a boat had been sent for him. In that case his mother was alive, and would welcome him. But if there was no boat, then a message from the gulf had been sent instead!

And there was no boat!—

For a moment his senses failed him; only confused sounds fell on his ear. But then he seemed to emerge from a dark passage. He must get to Hellebergene! He must see what had happened; he would go and search!

By this time it was growing dark. He went on shore and looked round for a boat as though half asleep. He could hardly speak, but he did not give in till he got the men together and hired the boat. He took the helm himself, and bade them row with all their might. He knew every peak in the grey twilight. They might depend on him, and row on without looking round. Soon they had passed the high land and were in among the islands. This time they did not come out to meet him; they all seemed gathered there to repel him. No boat had been sent; there was, therefore, nothing more for him to do here. No boat had been sent, because he had forfeited his place here. Like savage beasts, with bristles erect, the peaks and islands arrayed themselves against him. "Row on, my lads," he cried, for now arose again in him that dormant power which only manifested itself in his utmost need.

"How is it with you, my boy? I am growing weary. Courage, now, and forward!"

Again that voice outside himself—a man's voice. Was it his father's?

Whether or not it were his father's voice, here before his father's home he would struggle against Fate.

In man's direst necessity, what he has failed in and what he can do seem to encounter each other. And thus, just as the boat had cleared the point and the islands and was turning into the bay, he raised himself to his full height, and the boatmen looked at him in astonishment. He still grasped the rudder-lines, and looked as though he were about to meet an enemy. Or did he hear anything? was it the sound of oars?

Yes, they heard them now as well. From the strait near the inlet a boat was approaching them. She loomed large on the smooth surface of the water and shot swiftly along.

"Is that a boat from Hellebergene?" shouted Rafael. His voice shook.

"Yes," came a voice out of the darkness, and he recognised the bailiff's voice. "Is it Rafael?"

"Yes. Why did you not come before?"

"The telegram has only just arrived."

He sat down. He did not speak. He became suddenly incapable of uttering a word.

The other boat turned and followed them. Rafael nearly ran his boat on shore; he forgot that he was steering. Very soon they cleared the narrow passage which led into the inner bay, and rounded the last headland, and there!—there lay Hellebergene before them in a blaze of light! From cellar to attic, in every single window, it glowed, it streamed with light, and at that moment another light blazed out from the cairn on the hill-top.

It was thus that his mother greeted him. He sobbed; and the boatmen heard him, and at the same time noticed that it had grown suddenly light. They turned round, and were so engrossed in the spectacle that they forgot to row.

"Come! you must let me get on," was all that he could manage to say.

His sufferings were forgotten as he leapt from the boat. Nor did it disturb him that he did not meet his mother at the landing-place, or near the house, nor see her on the terrace. He simply rushed up the stairs and opened the door.

The candles in the windows gave but little light within. Indeed, something had been put in the windows for them to stand on, so that the interior was half in shadow. But he had come in from the semi-darkness. He looked round for her, but he heard some one crying at the other end of the room. There she sat, crouched in the farthest corner of the sofa, with her feet drawn up under her, as in old days when she was frightened. She did not stretch out her arms; she remained huddled together. But he bent over her, knelt down, laid his face on hers, wept with her. She had grown fragile, thin, haggard, ah! as though she could be blown away. She let him take her in his arms like a child and clasp her to his breast; let him caress and kiss her. Ah, how ethereal she had become! And those eyes, which at last he saw, now looked tearfully out from their large orbits, but more innocently than a bird from its nest. Over her broad forehead she had wound a large silk handkerchief in turban fashion. It hung down behind. She wished to conceal the thinness of her hair. He smiled to recognise her again in this. More spiritualised, more ethereal in her beauty, her innermost aspirations shone forth without effort. Her thin hands caressed his hair, and now she gazed into his eyes.

"Rafael, my Rafael!" She twined her arms round him and murmured welcome. But soon she raised her head and resumed a sitting posture. She wished to speak. He was beforehand with her.

"Forgive the letter," he whispered with beseeching eyes and voice, and hands upraised.

"I saw the distress of your soul," was the whispered answer, for it could not be spoken aloud. "And there was nothing to forgive," she added. She had laid her face against his again. "And it was quite true, Rafael," she murmured.

She must have passed through terrible days and nights here, he thought, before she could say that.

"Mother, mother! what a fearful time!"

Her little hand sought his: it was cold; it lay in his like an egg in a deserted nest. He warmed it and took the other as well.

"Was not the illumination splendid?" she said. And now her voice was like a child's.

He moved the screen which obstructed the light: he must see her better. He thought, when he saw the look of happiness in her face, if life looks so beautiful to her still, we shall have a long time together.

"If you had told me all that about Absalom, the picture which you made when you were told the story of David, Rafael; if you had only told me that before!" She paused, and her lips quivered.

"How could I tell it to you, mother, when I did not understand it myself?"

"The illumination—that must signify that I, too, understand. It ought to light you forward; do you not think so?"

A PAINFUL MEMORY FROM CHILDHOOD

I must have been somewhere about seven years old, when one Sunday afternoon a rumour reached the parsonage that, on that same day, two men, rowing past the Buggestrand in Eidsfjord, had discovered a woman who had fallen over a cliff, and had remained half lying, half hanging, close to the water's edge.

Before moving her, they tried to find out from her who had thrown her over.

It was thirty-five miles by water to the doctor's, and then an order for admission to the hospital had also to be procured. She had lain twenty-four hours before help reached her, and shortly afterwards she died. Before she breathed her last, she said it was Peer Hagbo who had done it. "But," she added, "they mustn't do him any harm."

Everybody knew that there had been an attachment between the girl, who was in service at Hagbo's, and the son of the house, and the shrewd ones instantly guessed why he wanted to get her out of the way.

I remember clearly the arrival of the news. It was, as I have said, on a Sunday afternoon, her death having occurred on the morning of the same day.

It was in the very middle of summer, when the whole place was flooded with sunshine and gladness. I remember how the light faded, faces turned to stone, the fjord grew dim, and village and forest shrank away into shadow. I remember that even the next day I felt as though a blow had been dealt to ordinary existence. I knew that I need not go to school. Men knocked off work, leaving everything just as it was, and sat down with idle hands. The women especially were paralysed: it was evident they felt themselves threatened, they even said as much. When strangers came to the parsonage their bearing and expression showed that the murder lay heavy on their minds, and they read the same story in us. We took each other's hands with a sense of remoteness. The murder was the only thing that was present with us. Whatever we talked of we seemed to hear of the murder in voice and word. The last consciousness at night and the first in the morning was that everything was unsettled, and that the joy of life was suddenly arrested, like the hands on a dial at a certain hour.

But by degrees the murder fell into its proper place among other interests; curiosity and gossip had made it commonplace. It was taken up, turned over, considered, picked at and pulled about, till it became simply "the last new thing." Soon we knew every detail of the relation between the murdered and the murderer. We knew who it was that Peer's mother had wanted him to marry; we knew the Hagbo family in and out, and their history for generations past.

When the magistrate came to the parsonage to institute the preliminary inquiry, the murder was merely an inexhaustible theme of conversation. But the next day when the bailiff and some other men appeared with the murderer, a new feeling took possession of me, a feeling of which I could not have imagined myself capable—an overpowering compassion. A young good-looking lad, well grown, slightly built, rather small than otherwise, with dark not very thick hair, with appealing eyes which were now downcast, with a clear voice, and about his whole personality a certain charm, almost refinement; a creature to associate with life, not death, with gladness, with gaiety. I was more sorry for him than I can say. The bailiff and the other people spoke kindly to him too, so they must have felt the same. Only the peppery little clerk came out with some hard words, but the accused stood cap in hand and made no answer.

He paced up and down the yard in his shirt sleeves—the day was very warm—with a flat cloth cap over his close-cut hair, and his hands in his trousers pockets, or toying restlessly with a piece of straw. The parsonage dog had found companions, and the youth followed the dog's frolic with his eyes, and gazed at the chickens and at us children as though he longed to be one of us. The girl's words, "But don't do him any harm," rang in my ears unceasingly—whether he walked about or stood still or sat down. I knew that he would certainly be beheaded, and, believing that it must be soon, I was filled with horror at the thought of his saying to himself, In a month I shall die—and then in a week—in a day—an hour... it must be utterly unendurable. I slipped behind him to see his neck, and just at that moment he lifted his hand up to it, a little brown hand; and I could not get rid of the thought that perhaps his fingers would come in the way when the axe was falling.

He and the warders were asked to come in and dine. I felt I must see if it were really possible for him to eat. Yes, he ate and chatted just like the rest, and for a time I forgot my terror. But no sooner was I outside again and alone than I fell to thinking of it with might and main, and it seemed to me very hard that her words, "But you mustn't do him any harm," should be so utterly disregarded. I felt I must go in and say as much to father. But he, slow and serious, and the clerk, little and dapper, were walking up and down the room deep in conversation, far, far above all my misery. I slipped out again, and stroked the coat which Peer had taken off.

The inquiry was held in my schoolroom. My master acted as secretary to the court, and I got leave to sit there and listen. For the matter of that, the clerk spoke in so loud a voice that it could be heard through the open window by every one in the place. The unfortunate youth was called upon to account for the entire day on which the murder had been committed—for every hour of that Sunday. He denied that he had killed her—denied it with the utmost emphasis: "It was not he who had done it." The magistrate's examination was both acutely and kindly conducted; Peer was moved to tears, but no confession could be drawn from him.

"This will be a long business, madam," said the magistrate to my mother when the first day's inquiry was over. But later in the evening Peer's sister came to the parsonage and remained with him all through the night. They were heard whispering and crying unceasingly. In the morning Peer was pale and silent; before the court he took all the blame upon himself.

The way it had happened, he explained, was that he had been her lover, and that his mother had strongly disapproved of the connection. So one Sunday as the girl, prayer-book in hand, was going to church, he met her in the wood. They sat down, and he asked if she intended to declare him the father of the child she was about to bear; for it was in this time of sore necessity that she was going to seek consolation in the church. She replied that she could accuse no one else. He spoke of the shame it would bring on him, and how annoyed his mother already was. Yes, yes, she knew that too well. His mother was very angry with her; and she thought it strange of Peer that he didn't stand up for her; he knew best whose fault it was that all this had happened. But Peer hinted that she had been compliant to others as well as to himself, and therefore he would not submit to being given out as the child's father. He tried to make her angry, but did not succeed, she was so gentle. He had an axe lying concealed in the heather near where he sat. He took it and struck her on the head from behind. She did not lose consciousness at once, but tried to defend herself while she begged for her life. He could give no clear account of what happened afterwards. It seemed almost as though he himself had lost consciousness. As to the other events, he accepted the account of them which had been given in the evidence against him.

His sister waited at the parsonage until he came from the examination, worn out and with eyes red with weeping. Once more they went aside and whispered. I remember nothing more of her than that she held her head down and wept a great deal.

It was in the winter that he was to be executed. The announcement was made at such short notice that every one in the house had to bestir himself—father was to deliver an exhortation at the place of execution, and the Dean, whose parishioner the condemned man was, together with the bailiff, had arranged to come to us the day before.

Peer and his warders and a friend, his instructor during the time of his imprisonment, schoolmaster Jakobsen, were to sleep down in the schoolhouse, which was part of the farm property belonging to the old parsonage. Meals were to be carried from our house to the prisoner and Jakobsen.

I remember that they came in the morning in two boat-loads from Molde: the Dean, the bailiff, the military escort, and the condemned man. But I had to sit in the old schoolhouse, and not even later in the day was I allowed to go down to where they were.

This prohibition made the whole proceeding the more mysterious. It grew dark early. The sea ran black against a whitish and in some places bare-swept beach. The ragged clouds chased each other across the sky. We were afraid a storm was coming on. Then one of the parsonage chimneys caught on fire, and most of the soldiers came rushing up to offer help. The great fire-ladder was brought from under the storehouse. It was unusually heavy and clumsy, so it was difficult to get it raised, till father broke into the midst of the crowd, ordered them all to stand back, and set it up by himself. This is still remembered in the parish; and also that the bailiff, an active little fellow, took a bucket in each hand and went up the ladder till he reached the turf roof. The black fjord, the hurrying clouds, the menace of the coming day, the blaze of the fire, the bustle and din…and then the silence afterwards! People whispered as they moved about the rooms and out in the yard, whence they looked down upon the schoolhouse-prison where the steady light burned.

Schoolmaster Jacobsen was sitting there now with his friend. They were singing and praying together, I heard from those who had been down in that direction. Peer's family came in the evening in a boat, went up to see him, and took leave of him. I heard how dauntless he was in his confidence that the next day he would be with God, and how beautifully he talked to his people, and especially how he begged them to take an affectionate greeting to his mother, and be good to her as long as she lived. Some said she had come in the boat with the rest, but would not go up to see him. That was not true, any more than that some of them were at the execution the next day, which was also reported.

I wakened the next morning under a weight of apprehension. The weather had changed and was fair now, but it felt oppressive nevertheless. No one spoke loud, and people said as little as possible. I was to be allowed to go with the rest and look on; so I made haste to find my tutor, whom I had been told not to leave. The two clergymen came out in their cassocks. We went down to the landing-place and rowed the first part of the way. The condemned man and his escort had gone on before, and waited at the place where we disembarked, in order to walk the latter part of the way to the place of execution, a kilometer or so distant. The execution had to take place at a cross-roads, and there was only one in the neighbourhood—namely, at Ejdsvaag, nearly seven miles away from where the murder was committed. The bailiff headed the procession, then came the soldiers, then the condemned man, with the Dean on one side and my father on the other, then Jacobsen and my tutor, with me between them, then some more people, followed by more soldiers. We walked cautiously along the slippery road. The clergyman talked constantly to the condemned man, who was now very pale. His eyes had grown gentle and weary and he said very little. My mother, who had been very kind to him, and whom he had thanked for all she had done, had sent him a bottle of wine to keep up his strength. The first time that my tutor offered him some, he looked at the clergyman as though asking if there were anything sinful in accepting it. My father quoted St. Paul's advice to Timothy, and instantly he drank off a long draught.

By the wayside stood people curious to see him, and they joined the procession as it passed along. Among them were some of his comrades, to whom he sorrowfully nodded. Once or twice he lifted his cap, the same flat one I had seen him in the first time. It was evident that his comrades had a regard for him; and I saw, too, some young women who were crying, and made no attempt to conceal it. He walked along with his hands clasped at his breast, probably praying.

We were all startled by the captain's loud and commonplace word of command, "Attention!" as we reached the appointed place. A body of soldiers stood drawn up in a hollow square, which closed in after admitting the bailiff, the clergyman, the condemned man, and a few besides, among whom was myself. A great silent crowd stood round, and over their heads one saw the mounted figure of the sheriff in his cocked hat. When the soldiers who came with us, having carried out various sharp words of command, had taken their places in the square, the further proceedings began by the sheriff's reading aloud the death sentence and the royal order for the execution.

The sheriff stationed himself directly in front of the place where some planed boards were laid over the grave. At one end of it stood the block. On the other side of the grave a platform had been erected, from which the Dean was to speak. Peer Hagbo knelt below on the step, with his face buried in his hands, close to the feet of his spiritual adviser. The Dean was of Danish birth, one of the many who, at the time of the separation, had chosen to make their home in Norway. His addresses were beautiful to read, but one couldn't always hear him, and least of all when he was moved, as was frequently the case. He shouted the first words very loud; then his head sank down between his shoulders, and he shook it without a pause while he closed his eyes and uttered some smothered sounds, catching his breath between them. The points of his tall shirt-collar, which reached to the middle of his ears (I have never since seen the like), stuck up on each side of the bare cropped head with the two double chins underneath, and the whole was framed between his shoulders, which, by long practice, he could raise much higher than other men. Those who did not know him—for to know him was to love him—could hardly keep from laughing. His speech was neither heard nor understood, but it was short. His emotion forced him to break it off suddenly. One thing alone we all understood: that he loved the pale young man whom he had prepared for death, and that he wished that all of us might go to our God as happy and confident as he who was to die to-day. When he stepped down they embraced each other for the last time. Peer gave his hand to my father and to a number besides, and then placed himself by his friend Jakobsen. The latter knew what this meant. He took off a kerchief and bound Peer's eyes, while we saw him whisper something to him and receive a whispered answer. Then a man came forward to bind Peer's hands behind his back, but he begged to be left free, and his prayer was granted. Then Jakobsen took him by the hand and led him forward. At the place where Peer was to kneel Jakobsen stopped short, and Peer slowly bent his knees. Jakobsen bent Peer's head down until it rested on the block; then he drew back and folded his hands. All this I saw, and also that a tall man came and took hold of Peer's neck, while a smaller man drew forth from a couple of folded towels a shining axe with a remarkably broad thin blade. It was then I turned away. I heard the captain's horrible "Present arms"; I heard some one praying "Our Father"—perhaps it was Peer himself—then a blow that sounded exactly as if it went into a great cabbage. At once I looked round again, and saw one leg kicking out, and a yard or two beyond the body lay the head, the mouth gasping and gasping as if for air.

The executioner's assistant sprang forward and took hold of it by the ends of the handkerchief that had bandaged the eyes, and threw it into the coffin beside the body, where it fell with a dull sound. The boards were laid over the coffined remains, and the whole hastily lifted up and lowered into the grave.

Then my father got up on the platform. Every one could understand what

HE said, and his powerful voice was heard to such a distance that even now it is remembered in the district. Following up the thunderous admonition of the execution itself, he warned the young against the vices which prevailed in the parish—against drunkenness, fighting, unchastity, and other misconduct. They must have liked the discourse very much, for it was stolen out of the pocket of his gown on the way home.

As for me, I left the place as sick at heart, as overwhelmed with horror, as if it were my turn to be executed next. Afterwards I compared notes with many others, who owned to exactly the same feeling. Father and the Dean dined at the captain's with the other officials; but they separated and went home directly after dinner.

Lector House believes that a society develops through a two-fold approach of continuous learning and adaptation, which is derived from the study of classic literary works spread across the historic timeline of literature records. Therefore, we aim at reviving, repairing and redeveloping all those inaccessible or damaged but historically as well as culturally important literature across subjects so that the future generations may have an opportunity to study and learn from past works to embark upon a journey of creating a better future.

This book is a result of an effort made by Lector House towards making a contribution to the preservation and repair of original ancient works which might hold historical significance to the approach of continuous learning across subjects.

HAPPY READING & LEARNING!

LECTOR HOUSE LLP
E-MAIL: lectorpublishing@gmail.com